Love Rehab

To Kimberly -
You rock! ♥ Jo Piazza

Love Rehab

a novel in twelve steps

JO PIAZZA

OPEN ROAD
INTEGRATED MEDIA
NEW YORK

Copyright © 2013 by Jo Piazza

Cover design by Mimi Bark

ISBN 978-1-4532-9507-6

Published in 2013 by Open Road Integrated Media
345 Hudson Street
New York, NY 10014
www.openroadmedia.com

*To all my ex-boyfriends for making me crazy and
all my girlfriends for making me sane again.*

Love Rehab

Admit you are powerless and your life is unmanageable

Annie and I hit rock bottom the same week. She sucked down enough tequila to incapacitate a three-hundred-pound sailor while I overdosed on a very bad man. Neither of us thought what we were doing was self-destructive until it became too, too obvious that it was.

Too, too obvious started on a Tuesday night in July.

I was curled into a human nest on the couch—legs crossed over each other, arms looped through bent knees, hair in a state of serious unwash—waiting for a reply text to a message I had sent hours earlier. I had resorted to playing childish games with the iPhone. If I turned off the ringer and flipped the phone upside down, then maybe I could force the appearance of a new message when I broke down and flipped it over . . . every thirty seconds.

I cleared out junk mail (those near-daily quivers you get from Match.com if you've even glanced sideways at their site in the past ten years) and old texts from my parents in the irrational hope that by creating space on the phone something new would appear.

The message I had sent, the one I was waiting for a reply to, was a pathetic kind of message begging for one more conversation to prolong the continuing breakup with my boyfriend, Eric—a breakup he desperately wanted and I didn't.

This breaking-up discussion began in person with me storming out of his apartment. It continued over exactly six and a half hours of phone calls that became increasingly more one-sided and had moved first to Gchats and now to text messaging—the devolution of a relationship in the digital age. It's funny how they always end the way they start out.

Our text messaging was all I had left.

See, even though I was the one to storm out of his apartment, I didn't want to break up. I thought the storming and the eruption would lead to some grand gesture or admission of undying love and devotion and a desire to move in together, buy rings, have babies.

It was pathetic, because I should not have wanted these things with this man. I had found a litany of e-mails between him and his assistant—dubbed by Annie (who, by the way, is my best friend), Floozy McSecretary (actual name Lacey, a complete bullshit name, which will henceforth not be repeated . . . because it sounds like a hooker name).

Why was I the one begging and pleading for our two-year relationship to continue another day when *he* was the one who cheated? I did tell you I was approaching rock bottom. I don't actually know where the phrase "rock bottom" comes from. Because I design children's books for a living, I have this tendency to illustrate certain phrases or situations in my head. I have always pictured "rock bottom" as a situation where your actual backside turns into a pile of rocks so heavy you can't move and are stuck in one horrible, really bad place, with a big pebbly behind! That kind of thing would weigh anyone down.

What I know now is that crazy "in love" people make bad decisions, and I was making my Eric decisions with my ass firmly implanted in a pair of bad idea jeans. I somehow convinced myself his cheating was my fault. I had been away from my real life in Manhattan for a whole month since my grandmother passed away. I was taking care of her estate back in my hometown in New Jersey (NOT THAT HE COULDN'T HAVE COME OUT TO NEW JERSEY!), trying to figure out what to do with a giant six-bedroom Victorian house with a widow's walk and wraparound veranda that needed about as much fixing up as my self-esteem. Grandma's entire block was like a lineup of discarded ex-girlfriends who had once been adored when they were shiny and new, and then turned in for something sleeker with more reliable plumbing. No one seemed to want giant six-bedroom old houses anymore in New Jersey. People in New Jersey all wanted the new style McMansion with its granite countertops, Sub-Zero fridges, and large breasts (I mean three-car garages). My parents had already semiretired to Florida and were clueless when it came to contracts and real estate. I think my grandmother's last joke on me was to bring me back to New Jersey and turn me into a spinster in her former house.

Grandma, who actually insisted that I refer to her as Eleanor in public because having a granddaughter meant you were old, was never a spinster even when she reached the proper age when one should actually be a spinster and surround herself with cats and crocheted things. Ever since my grandfather passed away when I was six, Eleanor was the Blanche Devereaux of our town, shacking up with every newly available widower as soon as they came onto the market. Men adored her. They simply doted on her with flowers and presents and trips to West Palm Beach.

Growing up watching her I got the impression that dating should be all about the man courting the woman and showering her with limitless attention.

That's definitely only true for senior citizens.

She would have hated the way I was plodding through the now dusty rooms like a modern-day Miss Havisham—if Miss Havisham had been partial to a hole-riddled Juicy Couture tracksuit that smelled like Doritos. A moth-eaten wedding dress would have been an improvement.

But as a I wore a groove into the wooden floors with all my plodding, I had developed some theories about why my relationship ended—eleven different theories in all to be exact (only two of which were outlined to Eric in detail over a series of text messages). My latest brainstorm was that the blame couldn't be put onto Floozy at all. I had seen enough episodes of Dr. Phil to know that cheating was always symptomatic of something gone wrong in a relationship. Floozy was a symptom. I was the problem. I was an absentee girlfriend. If only I had returned sooner and made my relationship a priority, then Floozy never would have been able to sink her acrylic French manicure into Eric.

Objectively I did understand what a red-blooded American man saw in Floozy. She was blond to my brunette, blue eyed to my murky hazel, big boobed to my modest B-cups, and twenty-three to my thirty. She wasn't shy about showing off her ample assets either. Before rock bottom swiftly approached along with the night of the unreturned text messages, back in the halcyon early days of our courtship, I would stop into Eric's Midtown hedge fund office for lunch and there they would be, Floozy's D-cups popping out of an assortment of unitards made of a material closely related to Saran Wrap. They were truly a wonder to behold. Given enough grappa I probably would have reached out and touched one. When I illustrated Floozy in my head—fairly often I caricatured the two of them together, often in peril—those boobs were so immense and disproportionate to her little blond head that she fell on her face, before being eaten by a lion.

I contend that you can tell a lot about people and what is most important to them by the first question they ask you when you meet them. I'm easy. I usually ask people how their day is going. It's boring, I know, but I actually *do* care what kind of day most people are having. I genuinely appreciate people being happy and feeling good.

There are the people who long for their teenage glory days,

who always ask you what high school you attended. This is often very important for people who went to high school where things like football were a big deal or for people who went to very fancy boarding schools in western Massachusetts.

Then there are the people who ask you where you went to college. This is more customary than high school and less specific (since who really cared that I went to Valley Green High in Yardville, New Jersey, home of the fighting Challengers, awkwardly named for the long-ago exploded space shuttle). College gives strangers a common ground. It lets people play the name game, which is always a nice icebreaker.

"Do you know Susie Goldberg?"

"Of course I know Susie Goldberg. She lived on my hall freshman year. She was so outgoing."

And then in hushed tones the other person adds: "Yeah, superoutgoing. Was she still a little bit of a . . . you know. Was she popular?"

"Oh my God, Susie totally got around freshman year. One time at a Phi Delt rush event, two guys and a midget stripper . . . "

And then you were clinking beer glasses and becoming shot-doing friends with this random person all because you were able to bond over Susie Goldberg (now a mother of two, happily living in Greenwich, CT) being a whore. The college question is a good one, except when associating with people from Harvard.

Harvard people like to say: "I went to school in Cambridge." Of course, everyone knows that means Harvard because there is only one school in Cambridge. The not saying of Harvard somehow becomes more pretentious than the saying of Harvard and then you have to hate that person. I once had hate sex with a guy who did the whole "I went to Cambridge" thing. He gave me crabs.

The first question Floozy asked me was where I went to the gym. I mumbled something about a Crunch, because seven years ago I had stopped in to activate a free monthly pass and taken an ill-fated Zumba class at the Crunch gym in the East Village. I don't care what Madonna says about the benefits of Zumba— white girls from New Jersey with two left feet shouldn't partake in the art of Brazilian dance. I could hardly sit down for a week.

Floozy was also always supernice to me, which made the betrayal part of this whole thing a little bit worse. Since she organized Eric's calendar, I knew it was her who remembered my birthday and sent daisies to my apartment (since I didn't like roses) and who made dinner reservations for my parents' anniversary.

What a bitch.

Around three in the morning, as my shame spiral was finally starting to settle in for the evening, and I teetered in and out of sleep, twitching at any vibration from the general direction of my phone, I was startled by the blue-and-red flashing lights of the town sheriff's car on the front lawn.

What time was it? Four a.m.? Shit. Eric had gotten a restraining order against me? I had only sent ten, maybe eleven messages in the last ten hours. One an hour. What's the statute for texts? Is it like wine? You can send one every sixty minutes and not increase your blood crazy level above the legal limit? It was hardly restraining order–worthy. I peeled myself away from the plastic-covered couch I was too lazy to de-plastic and almost fell on my face, my left leg asleep. The police car was parked askew in the driveway, and it didn't look like there was even anyone in it.

This was the beginning of a horror movie. Sad, sad rejected girl with ratty hair lured outside by fake police officer to be killed by mad man with a hook for a hand. I wasn't going to let that thought keep me from going outside. Captain Hook was currently the least of my adversaries. Mine were big-boobed, love-of-my-life-stealing administrative assistants. Besides, the pretty blondes are almost always the first killed in those kinds of movies. I was too dowdy to be taken out. If Floozy were here, she would have been fucked. I padded down the cobblestone walkway in bare feet without bothering to flick on the porch light. Getting closer, I saw a figure slumped over the steering wheel. Captain Hook took a nap before bludgeoning? Maybe he saw me in the window and decided I wasn't worth a bludgeon? God, my self-esteem was in the gutter.

Hook also had distinctive red curls that even in the streetlight screamed, "Fire, Danger, Step back or I'll cut you." I knew those curls. I had been braiding them into pigtails since I was seven years old.

I met Annie Capaletti in the second grade when she saved me from what could have been a completely embarrassing and wholly defining moment for me as the new girl in town.

My family had just moved to Yardville, New Jersey, from the Chicago suburbs. We had driven the fourteen-hour trip in a single day in our Ford minivan; our small family of four was helmed by a father who was too cheap to shell out $59 for an Econo Lodge. My brother and I were so cranky and ornery (remember this was back in the days before family cars had DVD players) that my mom broke her cardinal rule of not allowing us to eat fast food and let us have Happy Meals four times along the way. Those delicious burgers with their waxy yellow cheese and chicken nuggets in the shape of an old man's thumb quieted us down but also wreaked havoc on our faux-food virgin bellies. And so I sat in my first day of second grade with a grumbly, fussy stomach and no idea where the bathroom was in this new strange school building.

I held it in. I held it in all through the Pledge of Allegiance and roll call and when Miss Sherman called me in front of the class to introduce me. By that point I was shuffling from foot to foot as I smiled shyly, praying that Miss Sherman would pull me aside to show me around the school before we began the lessons for the day—making the bathroom tour a priority. But the completely clueless Miss Sherman just told me to take my seat.

That's when it happened. My stomach had different ideas than I did about how to impress my new classmates. Out escaped a low grumbly fart . . . the kind of fart that can brand you a freak from the second to the twelfth grade and ensure the boys call you something horrible like Flatulate Face, Air Poop, or Log Leaver into puberty and beyond. A cute redhead with pigtail braids and a smattering of freckles across her nose was the first to react. She looked at me for a split second just as the snickers began and she moved into action. She put the heels of her palms to the middle of her heart-shaped mouth and vibrated her lips against them making a *Pffffffffftttttttttttt!* sound almost identical to the one that came out of my other end. The entire class let out the laugh they had been about to release for the first noise and assumed Annie had just made them both. Miss Sherman stared down at the little redhead with a look of consternation.

"Miss Capaletti, I believe you know your way to the principal's office, don't you?" she brayed down at the girl.

"Sure do."

And with that Annie stood up, gave me a wink, and marched out of the classroom to collect her punishment. I later learned she was sentenced to an afternoon of clapping out erasers, a task she said she never really minded anyway because she got to snoop on the teachers in the lounge after class let out.

That particular day she heard Miss Sherman declare her love for Principal Nailer to the school nurse.

From then on I was completely indebted to and in love with Annie. We did everything together until I left Yardville for college at Villanova and she went to Boston for culinary school. But even after that we still saw each other on holidays and found ways to work together at the local waterpark on our summer vacations. Annie's job was actually to tell larger women they were too fat to fit down the waterslide. She reveled in it.

Annie was the first person I called when my mom told me

the news that my grandmother had died from a prolonged battle with colon cancer, and she had visited me almost every day that I had been staying in town.

How the hell did Annie end up in a police car? wasn't the first question to cross my mind. This wasn't even the craziest vehicle I had seen her commandeer for a joy ride—that would be Old Man Jenkins's John Deere tractor the night of our senior prom.

When I opened the door to nudge her awake, her head teetered forward and she vomited all over my bare feet. It had been weeks since I had a proper pedicure, but this was gross all the same.

The vomiting roused her a bit, which was good since I wasn't game for wading through what didn't end up on my toes to pull her from the car.

"Hi, Sophie," she said as if we were meeting for coffee on a Sunday afternoon and not four hours past midnight with one of us in a stolen municipal vehicle.

"Hi, Annie," I said back with the same nonchalance. "Whose car is this?"

She looked back and up, and I realized she didn't have a clue how she got there. She was just coming out of a blackout. Annie had been drinking a lot lately. She was the owner of the town's most beloved bar, so it didn't seem out of character for her to have more than ten cocktails in an evening and, unfortunately, more often than not, still drive herself the two miles home from the bar.

Her job, after all, was to entertain customers and keep them happy so they came back and kept drinking. No one liked a sober bar owner. They were the pedophile priests of the hospitality industry.

At that moment I finally felt the unmistakable buzz of my iPhone, coupled with my ringer, turned to loud, in case I had dozed off and nearly missed this last stream of communications. Now was not the time for "Rump Shaker," in the classical stylings of Wreckx-N-Effect, to be playing at maximum volume. I yanked it out of my pocket and stumbled through the pool of puke that had started to harden a little around my feet.

Eric (cell): You need to move on with your life. I've moved on with mine.

I instantaneously thought of a dozen things I could reply with. I could tell him I didn't need to move on with my life since I could forgive him and we could get through this and move on with our lives together. Before my fingers could stroke the buttons, an aftershock rumbled through Annie and she dry heaved—and then retched out of her mouth and onto my phone. Sometimes a higher power does give you signs.

"Come on." I pulled Annie's shoulder and dragged her out of the car, half carrying her into the house, tears streaming down my face and other bodily fluids down hers. She threw herself onto the couch I had just vacated, forcing a plasticky *POOOOOOT* sound. I went to the bathroom to clean my feet and phone and change into an appropriate pair of pajamas. I grabbed a damp towel and de-puked Annie as best I could, then perched on the floor, my back against the plastic. I picked up the phone to read the message again, and as I composed and recomposed exactly the perfect thing to say that would make Eric fall madly back in love with me the instant he read it, my eyes became heavy and I fell asleep with the phone in my hand.

The morning sun hit the east-facing living room windows around 6:30. If my eyes were puffy and my head pounding amid the smell of dry vomit I could only imagine what Annie was about to experience when she opened her eyes to greet the day. There was no point in postponing the inevitable. I prepared to wake her with a swift tug of her big toe when Eleanor's bellowing brass doorbell did the work for me.

"What the hell?" Annie gurgled before grabbing a pillow and pushing it down over her eyes. I managed to stand and looked out the window to see the police cruiser still parked askew in the driveway and two very pissed-off officers on my doorstep to match it. Apparently they had driven over in Annie's abandoned car.

"Get up, cowgirl. You're about to be corralled and you might want a change of clothes for this," I yelled over my shoulder. I knew these cops. I had known these cops since the third grade when Sergeant Chris Zucker had these horribly smelly feet that he let air out at his desk in Teva sandals, and everyone called Sergeant Alan Bress, Alan Breast, something that still made me giggle because Alan had an unfortunate pair of man boobs, impossible to conceal even in his blue uniform.

"Morning, Sophie," Chris said, crinkling his nose a little at the smell when I opened the door. "I think you have something that belongs to us." I had seen Chris a few times since I came home a month ago. He had been at Eleanor's wake. He came with his grandfather, who kissed my hand and told me the world, in Eleanor's passing, had lost one of the true great beauties.

"We were just giving her a place to park for the night, Officer," I said, smoothing down bangs that refused to settle against my forehead.

"She here?"

"Of course she is. She's getting cleaned up."

"Got our keys?"

"I believe they are still in the ignition."

"Great place for 'em."

"How'd she get them in the first place?" Now Alan, his chesticles straining against the brass buttons of his vest, looked sheepish and began playing with his imaginary bangs—the ones that were there before his receding hairline got the better of them.

"Alan made a bet with Annie and he lost," Chris chimed in for his partner.

"Darts?"

"What else?"

"Doesn't he know better than to challenge Annie on her home turf to her game?"

"I think Alan was a little tipsy himself. Anyway, he lost the bet."

"So he gave her his car?"

"No, no, she just asked to run the siren. She said she wasn't going to take it. But then she took it." It was pretty obvious that these two, despite being on duty, had also been partaking of beverages at the bar, which is why they didn't end up tracking Annie down until after the sun came up.

"Of course she did. It sounds like this is just as much Alan's fault as Annie's. I don't see any reason to haul her in."

Annie was famously good at darts. She had learned how to play while studying abroad in Prague, when a group of gangsters in her local pub took a liking to her because they had never seen a ginger before and took her under their wing. To pick up extra cash Annie worked with them hustling tourists who didn't think such a pretty American girl would be so good at hitting a bull's-eye or remaining standing while shooting bathtub vodka.

Chris looked down, and Alan shuffled his feet some more.

"There's the problem. Annie caused quite the path of destruction on her way over here. She took out two mailboxes, dented a fire hydrant, and ran over Ms. Dinkdorf's cat."

I put my hand to my mouth. "Fluffy!"

"Cat heaven. Half the town saw her rip shit barreling through the streets with that siren going. We've got to get her for DUI and destruction of private property or we are going to be held liable."

"So what are you going to do? Arrest her?"

"She can come to the station with us willingly and we'll have to charge her and we can tell the judge to go easy on her. She'll probably get probation and some alcohol education classes," Chris said. Then, dropping his tone to a conspiratorial whisper, he went on, "Which I don't think is necessarily a bad thing at this point. She's kind of outgrown adorable drunk, don't you think, Soph?"

"I hear you out there," Annie said, all of a sudden appearing and looking absolutely no worse for the wear from the night before. Serial abusers of alcohol never suffer the same hangovers as us moderate drinkers—the same way I imagine serial daters rarely experience the same kind of heartache that the serial monogamous person enjoys after a bad breakup. She had somehow found a washed pair of jeans and a violet button-down top that looked killer with her green eyes and fresh-from-the-shower hair. It's too bad Annie doesn't like boys like "that," because both the officers turned to mush when she strode over to them.

"Last I saw you I was getting my latest bull's-eye," she said, wrapping an arm around a red-faced Alan's formidable waist.

"Last I saw you, you were burning rubber on Decatur, siren blaring and Backstreet Boys on the radio." Now it was Annie's turn to go red. If I knew anything about my friend's tendency for blacking out, and at this point I knew a fair bit, it was that she had all her faculties about her until she hit some mysterious wall and then the rest of the night was a complete loss to her.

"You hauling me in?" Annie clasped her hands in front of her own waist with a coy smile, her embarrassment turned to obeisance in an instant.

"Get in your car, Annie, and we'll sort it all out at the station."

Annie and I rode to the police station together in silence.

The Yardville cop shack is a four-room affair with a reception area and tiny lobby containing a faded yellow couch that had seen better days back in the '70s, a drunk tank, where I knew Annie had ended up a couple of times before I came back to town, a bathroom, and an open area for the town's six cops and sheriff to do their desk work, which was minimal given the low level of exciting crime activity. I perched on the edge of the crusty old sofa waiting for Annie to emerge from the back, hopefully properly cowed after she had been filled in on the destruction she caused in the wee hours.

Cowed she wasn't.

"BULLSHIT! Probation? Rehab? I don't have a drinking problem!" Annie was stomping through the station like a rhinoceros on Red Bull.

"Annie, come on now," old Sheriff McNulty said in his grandfatherly tones, better suited for public radio than reading people their rights. "We called the judge and we can give you probation and rehab, and none of this will stay on your record once you do those things. You don't even have to go to court. He's doing you a favor, you know, because he was a friend of your dad."

"I. Don't. Need. Rehab."

I was starting to think that she did need some rehab, but I didn't know how to tell her they were right. I stood up and asked McNulty, "What kind of rehab are we talking about? Does she have to go away? Does she just have to go to meetings?"

"That's up to her and the judge. She needs to start by going to the town's AA meeting tomorrow night in the Presbyterian church basement. Then we can talk about options and we can try to figure something out."

Annie tossed me the keys to her MINI Cooper convertible in the parking lot.

"I don't drive stick," I shrieked, tossing them back.

"Figure it out. Suspended license, bitch."

Blerg! I hadn't touched a stick shift since high school when my boyfriend, Matt Siggman, got hopped up on whippets at a Dave Matthews concert (the first time he proved himself anything but boring and stone-faced sober) and I had to drive us home from Jones Beach in his Mustang convertible, the one he bought because he thought it made him look like Dylan McKay from *90210*. Matt had a real thing for *90210*. He had every episode on VHS. He recorded them himself and labeled each tape with a white label in sequential order from 1 to 27. He let me watch them all when I had mono, which was really nice of him, but also led to our inevitable breakup, when I lost tape number 11, the one of the summer before senior year where Brenda goes off to Paris with Donna and Dylan cheats on her with her best friend, Kelly Taylor. I always thought Kelly was such a skank for doing that. Kelly Taylor may have been my first encounter with a BTCBT (blonde that can't be trusted). Anyway, Matt broke my heart after number 11 went missing. We're on speaking terms these days, and when I've been home in the past few years, I've had a glass of wine over at the house he shares with his husband, Robert. The Dylan McKay thing should have tipped me off.

I grinded the gears all the way home. "How long is your license suspended?"

"Ninety days, or until I complete the outpatient rehabilitation program, the AA."

"Which is every week?"

"Pretty much."

"And not walkable and we live in a town with no public transportation."

"You have so much going on?"

That stung. I didn't. I was able to do my job as a children's book illustrator from the house, even though before Eleanor died and before the Eric situation turned me into a useless lump on the couch, I had faithfully gone into the office every day to meet with editors and authors and storyboard book ideas. I had initially taken two weeks off to deal with everything in New Jersey, but my boss had been understanding when I said I wanted to work from home to get everything in my life settled.

"I do have to work. I may be a depressive, pathetic shut-in who will die alone, but I have to work during the days and I don't know if I feel like being your personal chauffeur."

"Let's just go to this first meeting and we will figure it out," Annie said as she twiddled with the radio.

"We?"

"I can't go by myself, Sophie; come on, just come for moral support."

I resigned myself to doing exactly what Annie wanted since that is what I have done since we were eight years old.

"I need a drink," Annie said when we arrived, slamming her car door with a force she rarely showed on her delicate darling of a car.

21

Not what I wanted to hear. I'm sure you thought stealing the police car and the obsessive text messages were our rock bottoms. Not quite. Prepare for our rear ends to turn to stone.

Annie settled onto the couch with a bottle of Jack Daniel's. I hate any brown liquor, so I cracked open a bottle of pinot noir. Two hours later, *Love Actually* was on the television. It had been our go-to romantic comedy for years, I think because it gave you hope that true love could actually happen to just about anyone (even the British prime minister!) when you weren't even looking for it.

I made Annie stalk Eric's new girlfriend on Facebook. And then . . .

I was startled from my red-wine-induced stupor by "All I wanna do is zoom zoom and boom boom, just shake your . . ." My mouth felt spongy, and I had to run my tongue over my lips to make sure I could make words. I needed a new ring tone.

It was Eric.

This could be it. He was calling to apologize. Floozy had perished in a tragic treadmill accident at the gym and he was already waiting for me at Penn Station with flowers and balloons just like in the final scene of *Love Actually* when everyone meets their loved ones at the airport and you realize that love is indeed all around.

There was a really angry man on the other end of the line.

"Take it down, Sophie."

"What? Eric?"

"Take my penis off the Internet," he grunted with a bit of a panicked squeak at the end of the sentence that indicated he thought (no, *knew*) that he was dealing with a person who did not have her marbles intact.

Oh dear.

The night before came rushing back to me in a blur.

After I polished off a second bottle of wine, I made Annie help me make a list of why Eric was a terrible, horrible, no good, very bad man. Lists have always been helpful to me. I make them for just about everything, from what to buy at the grocery store to how to decide what to do on a weekend.

"What about the time he got back from Europe and insisted on double kissing everyone hello like he was a count or an Italian supermodel," I slurred.

"Or how he would never sit at the first table they seated him at in a restaurant," Annie added. "He would always make the waiter feel silly and then arbitrarily pick a different table to make him seem important and selective."

"Ooo, ooo, or how about how he never just said, 'Hey, these are my friends from college,' or 'These are my friends from high school'; he always had to say, 'These are my bros from Exeter.' "

Then Annie added the doozy that inspired us to do evil: "Remember how he went through that gross sexting phase where he used to send pictures of his penis to you all the time? Penises are so gross. No one should take pictures of them. They look like sea monsters ready to attack. Ughhhhh, it's a big reason I like girls."

Eric had only done that for a week when he learned that I was less than responsive to the modern love declaration of sexting. I tried, but I couldn't bring myself to take a picture of my lady bits and send them over the Internet. They also never looked good in their close-ups, no matter the lighting (and I tried lots of different lighting).

Of course Floozy did it all the time. I found the sexts the same day that I found the incriminating e-mails. It was like *Penthouse* Forum on his iPhone.

Oh, where are you?
I'm at my grandparents' house.
Look at my boobs.

Or

I'm in a very important meeting with the Japanese. Take a look at my hard, hard cock. Wouldn't you like this in your mouth right now?

Or

Tee hee, look who forgot to wear panties to the office.

Floozy never seemed to remember to wear panties to the office.

I mused to Annie. "If Miley Cyrus and former congressman

Anthony Weiner have taught us anything, isn't it that sexting will always be made public?"

"Not if you're not famous," Annie said.

"Everyone's a little bit famous these days." It's true. We live on Facebook and Twitter and Pinterest and LinkedIn. Everyone is a little bit famous to the people in their networks.

And then I had the idea—the very horrible idea, my true rock bottom.

"Let's make Eric's penis famous!"

Annie snorted. "I think in some circles it already is."

That would have made me nauseated if I didn't have an armor of 14 percent alcohol pinot noir and Chianti Classico protecting my feelings.

"Let's put his penis on the Internet." I jumped onto the couch and punched my fist into the air. "Let's put it on his Facebook page!"

Annie hated penises, but she loved a project and she was a wildly productive drunk. "No, no, let's give Eric's penis its own blog, Ericspenis.blogspot.com."

"I don't know how to make a blog."

"I do. I made one for the bar."

And at that Annie was on BlogSpot creating a user name for Ericspenis.blogspot.com (password: Not2Hard).

Then things got blurry. I remembered scrolling through my phone and finding a picture of Eric's lower torso, leg propped on a stool or a chair and completely average-sized penis poking up between two down-covered thighs. I remembered Annie uploading the picture and I remembered celebrating our creation by sending Eric an e-mail with the link. Then I remembered nothing.

"Who else did you send it to, Sophie? What the hell is wrong with you? Are you a tween girl? Are you a mean girl? A bully? Do you want to ruin my life?"

I was a mean girl. A mean, mean tween girl.

"We didn't send it to anyone else. I don't think we sent it to anyone else," I whispered.

"You don't *think*?"

I was furiously scrolling through my phone as fast as my hungover fingers would let me. Outbox.

To: Eric (Personal Mail)
From: Me
Take a looooook at this jerkface. www.ericspenis.blogspot.com
SophieSophiemi

P.S. I thought you'd be better endowed, Annie.

And that was it. That's all there was. It looked like that had been sent just as I passed out.

"Sophie, this is getting sick. I am going to have to call the cops."

"We'll take it down, Eric. Please don't call anyone. No one saw it. Please," I begged.

"Fine. But leave me the hell alone, Sophie. We had a good

thing for a while. I don't know why you can't leave it at that and find someone new. I don't owe you anything. Good-bye, Sophie."

"Good-bye, Eric," I said to a dial tone.

I could hear Annie hurling in the guest bathroom across the hall. I was sitting speechless on the bed, head still throbbing, feeling like my brain had somehow disconnected from the bone part of my skull when Annie walked into the room.

"I think I have problem. I need help," she said with a calm resignation.

"So do I, kiddo. So do I."

*Find something greater
than yourself to make you
sane again*

Annie's mandated AA meeting was in the basement of the Presbyterian church my parents went to for three weeks when I was ten years old. They thought church would be a productive thing for our family unit, but before we made it a month they came to the mutual decision that Dad's Sunday golf and Mom's time in the garden were a much more productive thing for the family unit. My brother, Jamie, and I were left to our own devices on the Lord's Day. Everyone was much happier; Dad's handicap dropped by three and the roses looked fantastic.

A small group of men huddled chain-smoking outside the side entrance to the basement. The tall, bald guy in the tweed coat with arm patches looked vaguely familiar, but it was dusk and the lighting was bad and I figured it wasn't polite to stare in these situations. I didn't know exactly what to expect. We have a lot of neuroses in my family. My dad is OCD, the kind where he has to touch a light switch every time he leaves the room and cut his meat up into exactly eight equal pieces before eating it. My mother was a hoarder before hoarding became a thing that people from the Oprah network came to your homes to fix with hugs and $20 containers from Crate & Barrel. Mom filled closet after closet with old art projects, magazines, horse-jumping ribbons, baby clothes, and dog toys. You name it, we had it tucked away somewhere in our house. She was finally "cured" of her hoarding when Dad bought their retirement house in Clearwater, Florida, and told her she could pack exactly three suitcases or stay in the old house with all the crap. Mom might have been a hoarder, but she wasn't stupid. She chose the beach over the stuff, and the garbage men had a heyday. We weren't normal or anything, but we never had an addict in the family, the kind who went to rehab or AA and could tell us about how it worked. But since it's anonymous, maybe we did and I never knew about it.

The stairs to the basement smelled like fresh coffee and stale smoke. I wasn't expecting to see chairs set up in a circle, a table of brightly colored donuts, or a decently attractive guy about our age eating a Boston cream.

He looked up a split second before I realized I stared too long. He had a dab of cream on his nose. He gave me this giant smile like he already knew me or something and started walking my way. He looked a little bit like Eric, which made the corners of my mouth turn upward before I remembered that Eric and I were no longer a couple and that he hated my guts

for putting his penis on the Internet. I felt a distinct pain in my left side directly under my rib in the top of my belly. What is in that space that causes that kind of physical reaction? Sometimes I wonder if my metaphorical heart isn't in my chest, if it's actually just behind my liver. When the Eric doppelgänger was two steps from being close enough to reach out and shake my hand, Annie grabbed my forearm hard and hissed in my ear, "Is that Dr. Jacobson?" Sure enough, Elbow Patches from the parking lot was coming down the stairs, and it was our pediatrician, the very same man who set my broken wrist when I jumped over a tennis court net in fourth grade, took my tonsils out, and prescribed me birth control without telling my parents when I turned sixteen. He looked at me with the same warm smile as Boston Cream, who had now turned his attention back to the coffee.

"Sophie, Annie," Dr. Jacobson said, giving us each a hug. Then I remembered where we were. Dr. Jacobson must be leading the meeting or something. There was no way he was an alcoholic.

"So good to have you girls. Call me Jack here." He took a green half-dollar out of his pocket. "Twelve years sober," he said as he brought it to his lips and gave it a chaste peck. He looked at me. "I'm glad you finally came."

As he walked away I looked at Annie. "He thinks I'm the alcoholic."

"You are the needy one."

"Well, how do I convince him it isn't me?"

"You don't. You can't now. It would be rude. It would be like saying 'I know you're an alcoholic, Dr. Jacobson, and I don't want to be in your little addict club.'"

Boston Cream began clearing his throat, which seemed to be a signal for everyone in the room to start taking seats in the circle of chairs that were obviously meant for people smaller than the adults gathered in the room. By the artwork on the walls, I was guessing this was where the church usually held Sunday school. On closer inspection, Boston Cream looked a lot less like Eric than I thought. His face was friendlier, less severe, and he had more crinkles around his eyes, which meant that he smiled more, or used fewer products. I happened to know that Eric used an eye cream before bed every night. It was lady eye cream, the very expensive La Mer kind that they raved about in *Vogue*. I never thought that was at all odd or strange when we were dating. I thought it was nice to be with a man who took care of himself. In hindsight it was a little dainty. Boston Cream also had a tiny crook in his nose that was saving him from being too handsome.

The white-haired woman next to me offered me a piece of gum. It tasted the way I imagined the inside of the woman's purse must have tasted, stale and dusty.

Boston Cream was up at the podium, which made him seem in charge.

"Hi, everyone," he said to the room.

"Hi," they chorused back in a singsong.

"I'm Joe, and I'm an alcoholic."

Of course he was, why did I think he was here? It was obvious that I was the only interloper. "I'm four months sober today." The entire room clapped and cheered, which was a nice touch. It is heartening to have people clap and cheer after everything you say. I could get into this alcoholic thing.

Joe led the group through something called the serenity prayer and then gave announcements. The church would be closed next week for a workshop so they would be switching the meeting to the public library; one of the AA members had been diagnosed with cancer and they would be taking donations for flowers. Then he opened up the room for discussion. This was when things got interesting.

First, a portly woman, who I thought I recognized from my mom's beauty salon when I used to go there with her to get our nails done more than a decade ago, stood up.

"My name is Rita, and I'm an alcoholic."

"Hi, Rita," the room chorused.

Then Rita got ten minutes just to talk. She told the room about her husband, Jim, and how he ignored her. She told us about her kids who were just entering teenagedom and becoming horrible monsters. She talked about her mother-in-law, Judy, who constantly told her that she wasn't as pretty or as smart as Jim's high school girlfriend and who last weekend actually invited said high school girlfriend over for a Sunday BBQ. *I hated Judy!* She said it all made her want to drink, but she prayed to her higher power every day to be strong. People kept nodding encouragement at all the appropriate moments. They passed her a tissue when she needed it, and when she was done, she was enveloped in a group hug. She thanked the group.

"I couldn't do any of this without all of you, " she murmured. I heard Annie groan not so much under her breath. I loved every second of it.

Then came Rob, who worked at the gas station. After being sober for ten years, Rob had a drink last week. It wasn't just one drink. Rob drank four six-packs after his hamster, Raul, had died.

"I just didn't know how to handle the grief," Rob said.

And on and on it went. People just stood up and they told their stories. Some of them were hilarious and some were sad. Some were hilarious *and* sad. The entire room laughed and cried and kept clapping for every single person who stood up and shared. And even when people had messed up like Rob did, everyone was still supportive. No one judged.

When we had heard five stories, Joe stood back up and announced that the group would like to hear from any new members. I looked at Annie. She lowered her eyes and gave her head a tiny shake.

I could feel Joe's eyes on the two of us, obviously the only newbies in this group.

I felt this intense compulsion to share with this group of people, to unburden myself from all the crazy emotions I'd been feeling for the past two weeks, to finally admit all my erratic behavior to someone besides Annie and three of my other girl-friends. Those girlfriends, I had noticed, were letting my calls go straight to voice mail much more often than usual. I had gotten into the habit of repeating myself and working Eric into conversations he did not belong in. The other day my friend Megan was talking about how she got a flat tire on the New Jersey turnpike and how Triple A wasn't allowed to come on the New Jersey turnpike so she had to wait three hours for a turnpike-sanctioned truck to come help her fix the tire.

"Eric doesn't even know how to change a tire," I blurted out. "One time we were in the Adirondacks and got a flat and I had to change it right there on the side of the road. That's pretty badass, right? A girl changing a tire on the side of the road? Why did he choose her, Meg? Why did he choose her over me? I'll bet she doesn't even know where the spare tire is!"

The other end just went silent.

The problem with getting up in this circle and unburdening myself was I wasn't an alcoholic.

But they did think I was. Dr. Jacobson apparently thought it was me and not Annie who had the problem. Who would it hurt just to talk a little and divest myself?

I made the split-second decision that it wouldn't hurt anybody at all.

So there I was, unburdening all over the place. I bent the truth a little. Every time I admitted to doing something crazy because of Eric, I just substituted Johnnie Walker for Eric. So Johnnie Walker made me cry myself to sleep every night and Johnnie Walker made me so depressed I hadn't been able to work in weeks and stacks of children's books desperately in need of illustrations were piling up on my desk. Johnnie Walker was the reason I cut my bangs myself the other night. I must have looked the part of a very sad sack (due in part to the aforementioned uneven bangs) because everyone kept nodding at all the right moments. At one point Rita grabbed my hand and gave it a tight squeeze. Annie's jaw was practically on the floor by the time I finally sat down amid a rousing round of applause. And here's the thing. Afterward I felt totally better. I felt the best I'd felt even before Eric dumped me, because I had to admit I hadn't felt very good for the last few months of our relationship anyway. I had been walking around with what felt like a rubber-band ball in the bottom of my gut, all the different bands pulled tighter and tighter. But the ball felt smaller now, lighter. I sat through the rest of the meeting with a goofy grin on my face. Annie had one too, but I knew it was just because she couldn't wait to lay into me for what I had done.

Joe stood back up at the end of the meeting and suggested everyone do the same and join hands. Annie's felt sweaty in mine, and I realized I hadn't held her hand or the hand of any adult whom I hadn't been actively sleeping with or trying to sleep with in about twenty years. The connection felt nice, and I gave Annie's rough palm a squeeze. To my surprise, she squeezed back.

We bowed our heads and said the serenity prayer again. This time I paid attention.

God, grant me the serenity
to accept the things I cannot change;
courage to change the things I can;
and wisdom to know the difference.

As the crowd dispersed Joe announced, "Remember, everyone, that I am available for one-on-one and group counseling sessions if anyone needs a little extra help this week." He walked over to Annie and me after that.

"Do you ladies want to grab a coffee or something?"

Annie immediately piped up. "Yeah, we can go to my bar."

Joe looked confused for a minute.

"That's a bad idea, Annie. We're alcoholics," I said pointedly. "Let's go to the diner down the street."

Joe followed Annie and me in his car. As soon as my door shut, Annie let it rip.

"What the hell were you doing in there? You've never drunk anything stronger than wine in your life, much less Johnnie freaking Walker? Were you making fun of me? What was it all about?"

"I wasn't making fun of anybody. I just, I just felt like unburdening myself is all. It's hard to be open about relationship stuff. Half your friends give you an 'I told you so,' the other half feel bad for you that you're thrown back into the pool of singledom and that your so-called marrying years have been wasted. Did I tell you that Candace Evans actually said that to me? She actually said, 'It's such a shame you and Eric broke up; aren't you mad at him for stealing your marrying years?' as if there is a specified time when I can get married and after that I turn into an unmarriable spinster."

"Candace's husband is gay, right?"

"Yeah, and they're trying for a baby." It was funny because it was tragic and true, and even though it makes me a bad person, sometimes someone else's misfortune does actually make you feel a little bit better.

"Babies and adventure vacations always fix a bad marriage. Stop listening to Candace Evans. Go on."

"So the one or two friends who sit and listen and put up with all your whining finally become so alienated by round five or six that they stop being your friends altogether. And they're right. They're exhausted. You become like a broken record. They've heard it all before and the story never changes. He still leaves. He is still a jerk. Your theories about why just get wilder and wilder. Maybe he's a commitment phobe. Maybe he's gay. Maybe he's a CIA agent. They've already told you all the same tropes to make you feel better. You're too good for him. He couldn't keep up with you. He needs a woman who makes him feel like more of a man. He has mommy issues. But eventually they don't want to tell you anything. Because they are exhausted by the subject. It feels good to be able to get in front of a room of strangers and just share without preconceived judgment or concern that they will hate me. I feel better."

Annie got quiet. "I can see that. I can also see why they say these meetings work for people with real addiction problems, but, Sophie, I don't think I can do this every day, not with all those people in there. Not with old customers from my bar and my goddamned kid doctor, for Christ's sake. I don't know if I have it in me to get up in front of that group and talk."

"Well, you heard Joe at the end of the meeting. I think he is some kind of doctor or counselor. Maybe you could do some one-on-one sessions with him."

"I have to. With him or someone else. My probation mandates that I see an addiction counselor and attend a group meeting for the next ninety days."

The ride was too short to talk about much else, and soon we were settled into a corner booth at Nell's Diner with three coffees and three slices of banana cream pie, Nell's specialty.

"Sophie, I was really inspired that you were able to be so open at your very first meeting," Joe said with one of the warmest smiles I have ever seen. That smile was so honest and so real that I couldn't keep up my perfidy.

"I'm not an alcoholic," I blurted before shoving a heaping spoonful of banana into my mouth so I couldn't say any more. The lines between Joe's eyebrows furrowed in confusion, moving them to the same side of his face as the crook in his nose, and the sides of Annie's mouth curled into an anticipatory smile.

I swallowed.

"Well, I may not be an alcoholic, but I think I am addicted to something more dangerous. I'm addicted to love." Annie was finally surprised, and her smirk now turned into interest. It felt good to say it. That's what I was. I was addicted to love (#Robert-PalmerWinning), to the idea of loving bad men and staying in bad relationships. "I am. Every time I said Johnnie Walker, I meant some boyfriend I had who made me act like a complete lunatic. It's a serious problem being a love addict."

Joe opened his mouth, closed it again, and then sucked a breath in through his nose. I steeled myself for a lecture and to be called a liar.

"So you listen to Dixie Chicks on repeat sober and cry for hours at a time? And watch, what did you call it, *Downton Abbey* for four days straight?" he asked, recalling some of the pathetic things I had mentioned doing while I was "drunk" in the meeting. When I looked up to meet his gaze, I saw he was trying to suppress a smile. I nodded.

"You did need to let it all out."

"I did!" Now I was leaning over and explaining with my hands, which is what I do when I get really excited. "I think we all need to talk about it. I think if women had a place to go when they get dumped or, worse, when they can't leave a relationship that is seriously unhealthy for them, it would really help their self-confidence and self-esteem. That was the great thing about the AA meeting. No one acted like they were better than anyone else. They just listened. That's all anybody wants. They just want to be listened to, and they want people to tell them that one day it is going to get better. One day they won't wake up feeling like crap anymore. I think we also want to know that other people have the same problems we do."

Now that I started on my rationale I couldn't stop.

"When you're going through a bad breakup or you're in a bad relationship, you have these blinders on where all you see is people in good relationships. Then you hate those people and feel even sorrier for yourself."

Finally finished, I heaved a sigh.

Joe nodded and gave me a smile that said we would revisit my crazy in just a bit. He looked to Annie. "And you?"

"Oh, I'm a drunk, a court-mandated drunk. Stole a cop car and banged up some mailboxes the other night, might have killed a cat."

Annie was exaggerating for effect. On our way home from the police station the only thing she had shown the least bit of remorse about was Fluffy. We had driven straight to Mrs. Dinkdorf's house to see after the feline and been assured that Fluffy did indeed have nine lives and had managed to dodge Annie's siren-blaring advance. She had simply run off into the woods to chase after a badger for the evening, sending Mrs. Dinkdorf into a panic and causing her to report Annie's shenanigans to the police.

"Worst of it is, I'm a functioning drunk and since I own a bar, it's an asset, not really a liability."

Annie came from a family of highly functioning alcoholics, all of whom functioned until it was too late. She never really knew her mom, who had left Yardville when Annie was six to pursue her dream of being an actress in Hollywood. But when we were kids, we would sometimes see her cast as "suburban mom" in commercials for kitchen cleaners and three-ply toilet paper. I don't know if Annie ever found it ironic that her mom left her life in the suburbs in order to portray one on television. It wasn't something she liked to talk about a whole lot.

Annie was then raised by her dad and his two brothers, long-confirmed bachelors and heavy drinking Irishmen who ran the town's best (only) bar. She grew up on a barstool and drank her first pint when she was ten. In the '80s it seemed more acceptable to give kids beer, back when you knew they weren't allergic to every peanut, egg, and gluten molecule under the sun.

Instead of becoming a tomboy, living with three men, Annie became the lady of the house (and the bar). She was cooking gourmet dinners by puberty and had dreams of someday turning the bar into a chic gastropub. That dream seemed like a possibility when she got a full scholarship to culinary school right after high school. Then in her second year, her dad's liver gave out. She came home for a semester to nurse him back to health, but a semester turned into four years. By the time he finally passed away, Annie was running the bar full-time and drinking almost as much as her dad had been.

"I heard about the cop car thing," Joe said with a little bit of awe in his tone. "You really blared the siren all the way home?"

"You know better than I do, buddy." Annie went on to explain that she didn't know if the AA meeting in town was the best idea for her to get sober. She told Joe how uncomfortable she felt being honest around all her parents' friends and, frankly, some of her customers.

This was nice. It was almost like we were old friends already. And Joe didn't hate me for being a lying AA party crasher.

"You know, Sophie," he began. "Now that I know you don't have a problem with alcohol, I can't really let you keep coming to the meetings. They're pretty strict. The lifelong AAers don't even like to let people with drug addictions come to the AA meetings; they insist they go to the NA, Narcotics Anonymous, meetings, even though addiction is addiction is addiction."

"It sounds like the AA lifers are kind of snobby."

Joe laughed. "Some of them are. But I do think you've hit on something. I think you need a support group. Why don't you start one? Call it LAA . . . Love Addicts Anonymous, or whatever you want to call it. And, Annie, since you have to attend some form of group therapy, those meetings could probably count toward your quota."

"And could you offer her one-on-one counseling?" I asked. "At the end of the meeting you said you give one-on-one counseling. Why do you do that, by the way? Are you a doctor?"

For the first time since we met him Joe looked sheepish and a little bit ashamed. "I am a doctor. Was a doctor, no, am a doctor. I was put on probation because of my drinking. And the counseling is part of the community service I have been doing to work toward having my full privileges back."

"You're a shrink?" I asked.

"I'm a shrink," he replied. That easy smile was back.

"So you can probably answer this. Are love addicts the same as sex addicts?" Not that I knew much about sex addicts, but I had read a story in *People* magazine about the husband of a famous actress going to some rehab center in the Rocky Mountains because he claimed that he had a sex addiction after she caught him in their Malibu beach house with identical twins who dressed as cats.

Joe laughed.

"It really isn't my area of expertise, but what I do know is that sex addicts are more attached to sexual behaviors and the high of conquering a new sexual partner. Once someone shows interest in them, they tend to run away. Love addicts are often more hooked on the intimacy. Both of them can be treated with group therapy, although we hear a lot more about sex addiction than love addiction. That's why I think your group could be so helpful, Sophie."

"OK, Dr. Joe, I might take you up on this plan," I said with genuine excitement.

Even Annie looked like she was into it. I think she would have been into anything that didn't involve having to talk about her drunken escapades with the man who took her tonsils out.

Love Addicts Anonymous officially began with a meeting of three over banana cream pies. Maybe, just maybe, something bigger than my own problems could restore me to sanity.

Make a decision to turn your life over to a higher power

I threw myself into creating Love Rehab with the same fervor I had thrown myself into convincing Eric to stay with me. To my delight, when I began investigating love addiction, I learned there was actually a canon of scholarly research on the subject, most of it penned by anthropologist Dr. Helen Fisher at Rutgers University.

Dr. Fisher wrote this book about the science of love, called *Why We Love*, where her research consisted of interviewing couples in various states of coupling. She found pairs who had just met and were still in that early, "can't keep their hands off each other in elevators and grocery store checkout lines" kind of lust, and she found couples who had been together for ten years and had three kids, a mortgage, and maybe a lover or two on the side. She found couples like Eric and me who had been together two or three years and were at that fight-or-flight turning point.

Then like a mad love scientist, she injected their brains with this dye that would allow the organ to light up in funny colors when she put them through an MRI machine. Once the subjects were in the machine the doctor asked them questions about how it felt to be in love and how they would feel if that love were to all of a sudden go away. She asked them to describe their lovers and tell her how they met.

This reminded me of how Eric and I met. Meeting narratives have always been paramount for me in the overarching story of a couple. Once I have nailed down the story in my head (and it changes the same way any story would as the rough edges are smoothed over with each and every retelling), I illustrate it in my mind like a graphic novel with word bubbles and lots of hearts and singing birds.

Eric and I met while I was on a first date with somebody else. See, I hadn't been totally sure that it was a first date, because dating these days is so vague. But I had been bantering back and forth with a friend of a friend for a while on e-mail, and when he asked me to go to a cocktail party his law firm was throwing, it sounded datey enough. But because I wasn't sure, I ended up asking my friends Emily and Dave (the most wonderful couple in the world who have been dating for seven years) to come along as buffers. My "date" apparently felt the same way about me, because he added a buffer of his own, a college buddy named Eric. Needless to say, the date and I didn't hit it off, but Eric and I talked and laughed all night. The chemistry was undeniable.

It would have been uncouth to go home together after that, but we soon began texting, then Gchatting, then talking on the phone at a high frequency (the evolution of the beginning of love in the digital age). When we finally went on our own first date months later, it felt like we were already in a comfortably long relationship. That might be why I slept with him on that first date. Over time I continued to illustrate our meet-cute to include the two of us locking eyes over the head of my original date and Eric being so smitten he had to pull his friend aside and ask if there were any possible way he could take his place. I didn't know if any of this really happened, but it made for a beautifully drawn story.

Fisher's findings from her MRI experiments were ground-breaking. She learned that people in the throes of romantic love (the early stages) experience the release of dopamine at the same levels as individuals addicted to cigarettes and even cocaine. Believing they were in love released a slew of these happy-feeling chemicals that actually did physically addict her study participants to the process.

Dr. Fisher hypothesized that when these chemicals were no longer accessible, or when the romantic relationship ceased or went through a trauma, a person went through the same kind of withdrawal as an actual drug addict, as the person fiended to get the happy chemicals back. That's why people going through breakups often experience depression and why their relationships become all they can think about, in the same way that addicts are consistently focused on where and how they can get their next fix. It is also why relationship trauma gives a person butterflies.

Butterflies are actually anxiety over something going wrong in a relationship. People feel them when someone doesn't call back or when they are uncertain about the person's intentions. And then when the person finally reciprocates, the one waiting gets that rush of happy chemicals, just like a first hit. Love as we experience it might just be a series of chemical reactions.

It couldn't have been more applicable to me. When Eric and I first started seeing each other, I would be frantic waiting for him to ask me out again. My stomach would wind into knots waiting to hear back from him and I was certain that it was because he was definitely the one. Why else would I have such an intense physical reaction? I remembered being so happy when he would finally make plans with me or the first time we spent a whole day together and he didn't suggest going back to his apartment that night. I felt such a rush of happiness that I knew, just *knew*, that this was true love.

And now that it was over, I kept trying to get a hit. I googled Eric and Floozy daily, hoping for some new tidbit about their lives together, something that would make me feel involved. I created new Twitter and Facebook accounts so I could follow and friend the Flooz. That was the worst of all because the girl was like the Huffington Post of social media. She updated and posted everything and anything that happened in her life. I was obsessed and transfixed. Floozy woke up every morning and went for a run at six a.m.

@BabyGrl14: Almost woke up the huni bunni on way for run. Not like he'd mind LOL.

She often described her shower routine and the products she used in great detail. It was through her Twitter feed that I learned Floozy harbored fantasies of being something much bigger than Eric's personal assistant. Floozy wanted to be a beauty blogger. She carefully described everything she used to clean and prettify her face, often with grammatical inaccuracies and mixed metaphors.

@BabyGrl14: It gets my goat up when a face cream doesn't do what it says it should. I mean I heard that it was grate right from the horse's mouth.

It was like a little stab in the eye every time Eric chose one of Floozy's painfully misspelled mixed metaphors over me.

They had a seemingly endless string of dates, which was also painful to watch. It seemed like Eric and I stopped "dating" fairly early on and were more content to stay home at night and order SeamlessWeb while watching *The Voice*. I took this as a sign that he wanted to settle in and just be himself and be comfortable around me. Maybe he was just bored?

Eric and Floozy went to the movies and dinners and bike rides and the beach. I felt sick. I literally woke up and went to bed nauseated, but I also felt that little rush and that thrill every time I learned a new piece of information because it made me feel like I was still, in some small way, connected to Eric. This kind of behavior, I realized, was one of the things LAA would have to battle against.

My research into the origins of love addiction coupled with my own crippling obsession only confirmed that LAA was something I needed to bring to the women of the tristate area . . . and to me.

But I was trying to figure out how to spread the word. At first I thought Facebook would be a good way to announce the meeting, and then I remembered the meeting was supposed to be anonymous. How did alcoholics all find one another so easily? Could they smell it on one another? Maybe they had some kind of secret code where they walked around gently placing their forefinger on their temple when they saw someone else they thought might be an alcoholic. I had to remind myself to ask Joe.

Love Addicts Anonymous would have to spread through word of mouth. Who did I know who had the most powerful mouth? I broached the question a week after our first meeting with Joe, sitting in that same diner with Annie and her cousin Dave.

Dave was an inspiration to make this work. The three of us had been friends since we were kids, and ironically, given the subject of our strategy meeting, he was one of the most hated men by the women of our town.

We still loved him, mostly because I had never found him attractive and he had never found a way to dick me over.

Dave wasn't at all hunky or movie-star-like, but he did get ladies. He was handsome in the face with really good hair. He actually walked into a fancy salon in the West Village in Manhattan one day and told the hairdresser that he wanted his hair to look like David Beckham's in the new Burger King commercials. Now most guys couldn't pull that off, but Dave could and his hair did bear a striking resemblance to the soccer player's, even if his abs did not. He was a little chubby around the middle, something he tried to hide with layers of button-down shirts, sweaters, and fleece vests. His numero uno asset was a biting sense of humor that could keep me in stitches for days and had caused many a woman to fall prey to his charms. He adhered closely to the 2005 book *The Game*, in which author Neil Strauss advises men that the surefire way to a woman's heart was "the neg," a device wherein a man first insults a woman to put her on the defensive. Then, when she is feeling low, he promptly compliments her to boost her self-esteem and then forever endears himself to her. I saw a woman make out with Dave about ten minutes into meeting him at a rooftop party in Philadelphia five years ago.

His sense of humor also often veered into the very wrong.

"We just have to lure people there with the promise of fun and healing, even though they don't know exactly what they're getting into," I said.

Dave countered, "That's pretty much what they told the Jews."

"Use Megan, obviously," Annie said, ignoring him the way she usually did. Annie had never met Megan O'Brien since Annie lived in Jersey and Megan was my editor at the children's book publishing house where I worked. The fact that Annie had heard so much about her was a testament to the force that was Megan. Megan knew everything about everyone, but she was so kind that when she told you something it never seemed like gossip. Instead it always seemed like she genuinely thought this was information you should have in your life so that you either didn't make the same mistakes or so that you could help whomever she was talking about.

For example: She was the one who told me that Candace Evans caught her husband looking at gay porn a week before their picture-perfect wedding in St. Maarten. When she told me, she didn't sound like she was quoting *US Weekly* or being vindictive; she made it sound like I should know in case Candace ever wanted to confide in me instead of undermining me, as was her wont when she said things like I had wasted away all my marrying years dating inappropriate men.

It was also a warning not to marry men you caught looking at gay porn.

In addition to trafficking in personal information, Megan was a Yellow Pages, Zagat, and beauty blog all rolled into one. Need an Italian restaurant in the Village with lighting dim enough your date won't see that big zit to the left of your nose? Spasso on Hudson and Perry. Need a nonjudgmental bikini waxer since you neglected to keep things tidy during that long-term relationship? Olga at Max Wax on Seventy-Fourth and Amsterdam. Just don't ask Olga about her Serbian boyfriend. She'll go on for hours. Also take a Xanax about an hour before you go. Don't have a scrip for Xanax? Dr. Karney on Fifty-Seventh and Madison had a light touch with the prescriptions. Megan had the answer for everything, and she would know exactly who should come to our meeting.

Megan didn't actually need our meeting since after getting divorced at thirty-four to a man she was still dear, dear friends with, she had completely given up the fantasy of a Prince Charming and was immune to any kind of love addiction. I didn't believe it at first. I thought everyone secretly wanted that fantasy, but Megan really didn't.

She has contented herself with dating a slew of really young, hot studs who she says fulfill her every wish in the bedroom and really, really rich older gentlemen with net worths in the hundred millions who fulfill her every wish at Bergdorf's.

"My requirement for a boyfriend these days is breathing and a jet," she told me last time we hung out over margaritas. She calls these men her Sally Tomatoes after the jailed mobster who paid Audrey Hepburn through his lawyer to pick up Sally's weekly weather report in *Breakfast at Tiffany's*. Thankfully for Megan she also doesn't see looks and finds much older (think Hugh Hefner, maybe even Kirk Douglas) men hilarious, charming, and chivalrous in a way that men of our generation never are. Megan wouldn't be attending our meeting, but she would make sure that the right people heard about it.

The next problem was location. In Manhattan we would have to rent a space, and space is a premium commodity in New York City.

"We can do it at your house," Annie said. "It's like a five-minute walk from the NJ Transit stop and it's only a half-hour ride out here. Everyone loves leaving the city."

Although I didn't really believe people actually liked commuting out of New York, I was surprised and happy that Annie was getting behind this idea. I think she would have done anything not to go back to that AA meeting with Dr. Jacobson.

I was about to agree when I saw a familiar sandy-blond head at the counter.

"Hey, Joe!" I waved. He turned around holding a tin of banana cream pie.

"Hey, Sophie," he smiled sheepishly. "I guess you got me hooked." He nodded down to the pie.

"Are you going to eat that whole thing by yourself?" I asked, realizing only as I asked it that I was not at all casually asking if he was taking the pie home to a girlfriend (no ring, no wife).

"I have a friend coming over tonight," he said with a smile. Of course he did. She was probably another doctor at the hospital who looked exactly like Addison Montgomery on *Private Practice*. I was drawing a picture of them in my mind, cuddled on the couch talking about hilarious hospital drama while feeding each other my banana cream pie.

"Hey, Sophie, are you OK?" Joe asked. I had spaced. God, I needed LAA. I needed something. I was getting jealous of a potential girlfriend of a man I had once shared a slice of banana cream pie with after lying to him at his Alcoholics Anonymous meeting. I was so far from normal. Not for the first time since I had moved home I envied my grandmother's love life. Not only did she find her soul mate in my grandfather, but when he finally passed on, she just flitted from man to man without a care or a regret in the world. She just had it figured out.

"I'm great. I was having inappropriate thoughts about pie." Ohmygawd, what did that even mean? "I mean about, you know, eating it."

"Yeah, I can't wait to get this one home. Give me a ring after your first LAA meeting." Joe smiled warmly as I gave a little wave.

"Was that the infamous Dr. Alchy?" Dave asked.

"It was."

"He looks like a nerd."

Annie threw a napkin at him. "Why do you hate everyone? You hate women, you mock men. Sometimes I think you are a self-hating gay!"

Dave shrugged. "I like vagina. So can I come to your meeting?"

"Dude, that's like inviting Jose Cuervo to AA. You're the problem, Dave. You're the one who drives these girls bananas," Annie said.

Dave couldn't deny it. He was a serial womanizer and he simply treated women like shit, which often made them simultaneously hate him and continue coming back for more. He once admitted to us that when one woman asked him what he liked about her, he told her she was brunette and had a vagina. He was inside her at the time. And as if to underscore the point, our waitress, Maggie, dropped the bill on our table and with no regard for how her tip would fare, she picked up a half-empty glass of Coke and splashed it in Dave's face.

"Fuck you," she said and walked away.

"What a turkey," Dave muttered.

"See," Annie said. "You can't come."

We called Megan and told her about the meeting, set it for the following Sunday, and asked her to spread the word. Megan said she knew at least ten women currently in the throes of some kind of love addiction. She also gave me a hot tip on a Diane von Furstenberg sample sale taking place the following Thursday.

Sunday is a good day to make plans with other single women because it is such a bad day for them. On Sundays couples sleep in late, wake up and have missionary morning sex, and then brunch before heading to Home Depot to pick out new blinds or area rugs for the apartment they just moved into together. For singles, Sunday is waking up with a hangover, maybe a strange man in your bed, figuring out how to get said strange man out of your bed, and then sending a dozen text messages to your other still-single friends to see who wants to have brunch with you somewhere they have unlimited Bloody Marys because, one, you're footing the bill; two, you need to get a little drunk to erase the pain of not having someone to go to Home Depot with; and, three, you woke up with a strange man in your bed and you are already bummed that he didn't want to have brunch and hasn't texted you.

We didn't invite Joe to the meeting. We thought it would be strange to have a guy there even though we never specifically said that LAA was for women only. Men nurse broken hearts too. But still, they do it in a different way than women. At least that's what I thought at the time.

Come Saturday night I was cooking dinner for Annie and me. She had pretty much moved into one of the spare bedrooms in my grandmother's house and had turned over her duties at the bar to her assistant manager, Fredo. We were a de facto sexless couple. I would cook. She would complain. I would clean. She would make things messy. It was like most hetero relationships after about a year. But even Annie couldn't listen to me talk about

Eric anymore. When I began recounting his day with Floozy from memory and asking her what she thought it all meant for maybe the hundredth time, she calmly strode across the kitchen.

"Put down the spoon, Sophie." She nodded to the utensil I had been using to smash potatoes.

"They're almost smashed," I replied. "So then I think they went to the High Line with his sister and her two kids because Floozy took an Instagram . . . OUCH!"

Annie had slapped me. She used her open palm to slap me across the face. I had never been hit before. My first instinct to lunge at her was quickly replaced by an urge to cry and feel horrible for myself, but Annie wasn't giving me the opportunity to have those kinds of feelings.

"I need you to shut the fuck up about Eric and Floozy Mc— WHAT THE FUCK IS HER REAL NAME?" Annie bellowed. "You need to shut the fuck up."

I squared my shoulders and rolled my eyes to the ceiling before responding to her.

"I'm going to try. I want to try."

Annie was already at the freezer searching for a bag of something frozen to put on my face.

"Will a Skinny Cow work?" She calmly offered me a low-calorie ice cream treat. I took it without saying anything.

She breathed deeply. "I want the old Sophie back. You have become a crazy person who is fixated on a single thing, a thing, I might add, that is poisonous for you. I understand the irony of the alcoholic in the room saying that. Yes, this may be the pot calling the kettle an addict, but I just want my friend back."

I didn't have anything to say. She was right. I gave her a nod and headed upstairs to my room.

In bed that night, thinking about the LAA meeting, I was nervous and my face stung. What if no one showed? Megan told me a lot of women said it sounded like a good idea, but New York ladies are naturally flaky. They love everything in theory, but trying to get them to do anything that doesn't involve booze and men and does involve trains and New Jersey is hard. I sat awake until three in the morning, wondering if we would have an empty house on Sunday. I was pegging this meeting to lifting my spirits and giving me something to focus on besides my horrible, no good, very bad love life. I really didn't want Annie to hit me again, but more than that I didn't want Annie to hate me. I was starting to hate me a little. I understood the irony of all this planning. Lifting my spirits involved an event whereby I was going to sit for a couple of hours and talk about my terrible, no good, very bad love life. I wanted to talk more with Annie about it, but I was a little bit afraid of her. Plus Annie was sleeping like a baby. She would do that for at least four hours at a time, then she would wake up and pace on the back porch with a cigarette. Chain-smoking had become a new addiction for her, but I was happy to let her substitute the lesser of two evils. Cigarettes didn't make her steal cars.

I did my hair for the first time in a month on Sunday morning, curling it under at the ends. I willed myself not to look at

Floozy's Twitter feed. I plucked a few stray eyebrows, vowing to get them waxed next time I went into the city, and put on what I thought was rehab chic: skinny jeans with a cozy Tucker cardigan. Comfort was something I imagined people in rehab would embrace.

I checked her Facebook, just once.

Noon came and went without anyone arriving. And 12:20 and 12:30, and finally at 12:45 the doorbell rang. Then it just kept ringing so I finally had to leave it open. I had assembled every chair in the house in a circle in the living room. Thirty seats in all. And by 1:00 p.m. they were all filled. Sure, everyone was a little late, but they had come. A lot of people had come. Some of the women I knew. I recognized Olivia as one of Megan's many cousins. (Megan's family is very Irish Catholic and by her own admission they breed like rabbits.) Cameron was a girl I had gone to college with whom I had e-mailed toward the end of the week when I got spooked that no one would show. We saw each other socially and tried to have a drunk Sunday brunch once or twice a year, and each time we met she regaled me with stories about another man who had done her wrong whom she desperately wanted to marry and have babies with. One of the women I didn't recognize was an enormous Indian girl, who introduced herself as Prithi. She was swathed in several of her own long cardigans. (I gave myself a pat on the back for our shared sartorial sense.) Prithi practically had to waddle to her seat.

I got up in front of the group the way Joe had at the AA meeting. "Welcome to the very first meeting of Love Addicts Anonymous," I said, my voice shaking a little from nerves. I balled the ends of my cardigan up in my hands and kneaded them across my sweaty palms. "This is a safe place." Joe had instructed me to use that introduction even though it sounded a little creepy, along the lines of "show me on the doll where he touched you." "We're all here because we recognize a problem in ourselves and we want to try to fix it. I think women give themselves a bad rap. We're always competing with one another instead of helping each other out, when we all go through the same things. This is a chance for us to get together and help one another through a tough time." Looking at the hopeful and somewhat needy expressions of the women in the audience gave me a sense of confidence. I felt stronger now and more sure of myself.

"Let's face it; our friends and family are sick of hearing us whine about our crappy relationships. There are some things we do that are so crazy we don't even tell our friends, and then we feel guilty about it because it's our secret crazy. All those fake e-mail accounts we create to send one last message and times we've just happened to end up in the same bar because we've stalked a status update—that's shit no one likes to admit to anyone else. Now we're in a space where we have license to whine and admit the secret crazy, and the goal is that by talking about these things we won't make the same mistake twice. We need to break our cycle of love addiction. We too can be those carefree women who live and love and go on to love again without going to a dark place." In my head whenever I pictured this kind of woman she was always like one of those ladies in the Tampax commercials who were carefree and easy breezy running on a beach. Not only did her heart never get broken, but she also never bled through her white pants.

I walked away from the front of the room right after I stopped talking and was caught off guard by the spontaneous applause that erupted from the group. Had these people been to AA before or was this some kind of ingrained group dynamic? Whatever it was, it felt good; my spine grew an inch longer, and I stood a little taller before taking my seat. I had never gotten applause all for myself before.

I told my own story about how I caught Eric cheating with Floozy and staged my pathetic faux breakup in his apartment. I continued through the sad weeks of calling and texting and culminated with the man bits ending up on the Internet.

The room agreed that breaking up with someone to try to force them to (a) become more serious or (b) stop doing something hurtful to you just about never works. That seemed like a good rule to remember.

Rule 1: Staging a dramatic outburst never leads to a grand gesture.

We went around the circle and everyone shared just like they had in the AA meeting, except each of these women's stories involved some kind of neurosis about men and relationships.

Everyone started out by putting their hands in the air, saying their name and "I'm a love addict," like we had seen people do in the movies. It made us giggle at first, but I have to admit there was something therapeutic about saying it out loud.

Cameron: Was addicted to online dating, despite several disastrous dates that resulted from her efforts on Match.com, J-Date, and something called A Lot of Fish. Among these disasters was Vegan Biter. In his online profile on A Lot of Fish, Matthew had seemed totally datable. He was a lawyer, living in Brooklyn, nonsmoker, social drinker, liked travel, loved animals. When they got to the bar, Cameron found out that Matthew loved animals so much he didn't eat them. Cameron let this go despite her own near addiction to medium-rare hamburgers with blue cheese and continued with the date. Over the next three hours, Matthew told her he was from Staten Island, his dad was a racist, his sister had two illegitimate children, he never went in the ocean because he was afraid of sharks, and he didn't fly because he was afraid of planes. "I thought you said in your profile you liked to travel?" Cameron asked. "I've driven to Disney World seven times. Have you been to Epcot? It's like seeing the whole world without getting on a plane," he said.

When Cameron told him maybe he was sharing too much for a first date, he replied, "Wouldn't you rather have everything out on the table at the very start of things?" Since this seemed entirely rational, Cameron agreed and kept drinking dirty martinis, maybe a little faster than before. He invited her back to his place to see his fish. He wouldn't shut up about his damn fish, and against her better judgment she went. She blamed the gin and the fact that he promised some of his fish glowed in the dark. They did indeed glow in the dark and before Cameron knew it they were making out by the light of the glow-in-the-dark fish in the bedroom of his junior one-bedroom in Chelsea. That's when he started biting. The first one was right above her left hip and it was a sizable bite. Cameron bruised easily and yelped, "Hey, cut it out." And he did for about ten minutes until he got his teeth close to the fleshy part of her thigh and then, CHOMP! That was the last straw, and Cameron called it a night. She couldn't wear a bikini for weeks while the welts healed.

Annie got a good laugh at that one.

"He was hungry. He hadn't had protein in nine years!!!!"

The other online outcasts Cameron picked up included a banker who brought his mom along on their first date, a television producer who she caught wearing her black La Perla panties after he spent the night at her apartment, and the dog walker who left a Chihuahua at her house and never returned her calls. She calls him Paco. He was in her purse. Still Cameron kept at it. And the worst part was that she was never the one to call a spade a spade. She usually stuck around until they stopped calling or texting or erupted in an admission of hatred.

Melissa: Five months ago her husband, a doctor in Manhattan, cheated on her with one of the nurses in his hospital. She found out because another nurse, in a fit of altruism or maybe smuggery, e-mailed her about it. When she confronted him, he didn't deny it, and since it was the second time she had caught him cheating, she was finally ready to kick him to the curb and she told him she wanted to file for divorce. She may have been ready to end her marriage, but she certainly wasn't finished talking about it. She began nearly every conversation with everyone she met, "I don't know if you've heard but I'm going through a tough time. I found out my husband was cheating on me," and from there she would launch into the entire torrid story, sometimes varying the details. Occasionally she would mention how she left the other woman a birthday card on her windshield that said "Happy Birthday" on the front and "You Dirty Whore!" on the inside. Other times she would talk about how her two boys, Chase and Brandon, were holding up, or the latest thing that Dr. Mike had told her in therapy. She finally realized she might need to seek some kind of help when she pulled up to the gas station last week and, when Fred the attendant asked her if she wanted unleaded or regular, she said, "Fred, I don't know if you've heard," and he cut her off screaming, "Of course we've heard and I don't think that birthday card you left on that poor woman's car was the right thing to do!"

Lila: Pretended she was Jewish for a whole year because the guy she believed would be the perfect husband told her on their second date that he would only marry a Jew. She was and to this day remains a lapsed Southern Baptist. But Lila eagerly attended services and spent the high holidays with Ben Greenberg's mother and father. She was so desperate to get a ring that she created a backstory that included her taking a trip with Birthright Israel, something she learned about when she put "dating a Jew" into Google. She was in so deep she didn't know how she would ever get herself out of it. She figured they were so in love she could tell him and they would have a good laugh, she'd convert, and they could still live happily ever after. They moved in together, they put a mezuzah over their door, and then, unexpectedly, her not-at-all-lapsed Southern Baptist parents dropped in for a visit, arriving on her doorstep asking what that little doll was hanging from her door frame, thus outing her as a shiksa. She and Ben Greenberg did not have a good laugh, and she was now couch surfing among her work colleagues.

Olivia: Had a habit of blacking out during her dates. Dating made her so nervous that she drank to excess, which she realized was a problem when she went home with one guy last week and in the middle of the night got up to take a pee and ended up in his roommate's bed—naked. She didn't notice a thing until she spooned him and he screamed. Her date came running down the hall. When she finally came to, she realized she didn't recognize either man.

Annie whispered something in her ear and Olivia nodded. I saw her slip her Joe's number and the address of the AA meeting. I was proud of her for wanting to take Olivia to an AA meeting and also a little proud of me (back pat) for doing something that was actually helping other people.

Allison: Was also desperate to get married. (This felt like a recurring theme, and I wasn't sure what to do about it.) She had been dating Alex for six years, since they graduated from college. They moved in together a year ago and Allison couldn't understand why he hadn't just popped the question yet. She tried giving him an ultimatum last April. Nothing. She tried withholding sex. He took longer showers. She tried talking to his mother. He just stopped taking his mom's calls.

"I was so frantic I thought about pulling the goalie. I was just about to stop taking the pill when I heard about this meeting." Allison laughed. "I guess that would have made me pretty desperate."

At that the girthy Indian girl with the waddle pulled back her long cardigan to reveal a very pregnant belly.

"I'm Prithi, and I'm desperate," she said, holding one hand in the air, the other on her massively pregnant belly. I made a mental note not to assume people are just fat. Of course it is better than assuming someone is pregnant, since calling someone pregnant when they are not in fact pregnant is tantamount to calling them fat anyway.

Prithi was born in the United States, but her parents were strict Brahmans from Calcutta. Since the time Prithi was a toddler her mom and dad had arranged for her to marry the six-months-younger son of their former neighbor in Calcutta, also a Brahman. He was an engineer who came over to the States when he was eighteen and attended MIT. When Prithi and Sasank finally met at age twenty, they hit it off. The problem was that they hit it off as wonderful pals. Sasank was the most intuitive man Prithi had ever met, and gorgeous. He dressed like a celebrity and his skin was as smooth as mahogany-colored butter. But he never made a move on Prithi. One night while he painted her toenails in her dorm room at Brown (his idea), he revealed that he thought he might be gay and that he was in love with a physics major named Michael. He told Prithi he would go through with the marriage because he really did love her as a friend, but he couldn't bring himself to consummate his relationship with her. Prithi also loved this man as her best friend, but she had to admit she had never been sexually attracted to him, either. They didn't have the hearts to break it to their parents yet, especially Sasank, so Prithi went out determined to find another suitable Indian man to marry who would please her parents and soften the blow. She met Dr. Amir Mehti the next summer when she was visiting NYU med school to decide whether she wanted to apply to go there. He was perfect—thirty-five, a cardiac surgeon, parents who still lived in Calcutta, his own apartment on the Upper West Side of Manhattan and a summerhouse in Montauk. Prithi fell head over heels and knew this was the guy she had to marry. He would make her parents so happy, and if they were happy, they might be able to help soothe Sasank's parents when he finally told them he was gay.

Prithi and Dr. Mehti dated through the summer and then he grew distant. She was desperate.

"If you think a good man is hard to find, a good Indian man is impossible," she said with a sigh at this point in the story.

As her desperation grew so did a plan, hatched by a joke Sasank had made in passing during their hours of chatting on the phone late at night.

"Just get pregnant. No honorable Indian man will leave a pregnant woman," he said, laughing. Prithi laughed too, but the next week she stopped taking birth control. At this point the good doctor was only returning one of every three of her calls. She got demanding about setting a date for them to go out and when it finally came around, she pulled out all the stops. She bought something called the water bra from Victoria's Secret that gave her cleavage nature had never intended. She packaged her newfound assets in a slinky bandage dress from Max Azria and shoved her feet into six-inch heels. Her seduction measures worked, and the doctor could barely keep his hands to himself through the appetizer. By the time he choked down his roast chicken, he had his hand halfway up her tiny skirt and was practically licking her neck as he breathed into her ear that he needed to have her right then and there. They got up from their table and slipped cautiously into the single-stall bathroom of the swanky downtown restaurant and Prithi had what she attests was the greatest orgasm of her life.

It was a hearty orgasm on all fronts, and four weeks later Prithi missed her period. She had also maintained her meticulous grooming regimen and now had the doctor eating out of her hand. Then she dropped the bomb. She was pregnant! He was shocked and a little terrified. He wasn't ready to settle down. He asked if she was keeping it. She nodded. There was nothing he could do. Sasank was right; good Indian men married the women who were having their children. Dr. Mehti proposed, albeit reluctantly.

"Will you?" he asked, as he handed over the requisite ruby ring his grandmother had given him to give his bride, a month after she told him she was expecting. Prithi screamed with delight. "I will!" She knew the doctor was just scared and he would come around once they were settled into their life together. She called her parents, and though they were upset about Sasank, they saw the doctor as a major upgrade. Doctor definitely trumped engineer. They also weren't pleased about the little blessing coming their way, now seven months down the road, but since a wedding was in the works they couldn't complain too much. Besides, her mother said, "We are a modern family."

By Prithi's second trimester in June she barely saw the doctor, even though she had moved into his Upper West Side bachelor pad. But she contented herself by finishing her applications to med school and looking for a new family-friendly town house in Brooklyn.

Then, last week, the doctor told her he couldn't do it. He was in love with someone else, a brain surgeon at Columbia whom he had been seeing before Prithi and had apparently taken up with again after she stopped wearing that water bra (it had burst when her real breasts started swelling, causing quite a scene at the home of one of Dr. Mehti's hospital's major donors).

He told Prithi he was calling off the wedding.

"Holy Mary Louise Parker," Allison whistled.

"Tell me about it," Prithi agreed. "And that surgeon isn't even as cute as Claire Danes, but she does have that evil pointy chin."

The entire group agreed, Claire Danes's pointy chin foreshadowed a certain man-stealing temptress who could convince a man to leave his eight-months-pregnant fiancée.

Prithi moved downtown with Sasank, who was now living

with Michael in a loft in Soho. And then she heard about the meeting and she got on the train to New Jersey.

"I can't face my family," she said through tears. "I can't go home. I have no job. I got accepted to Einstein for next fall, but how can I go as a single mother? And I can't keep staying on Sasank's bed. He and Michael need their space and a proper place to sleep and have sex since they would never kick a giant pregnant beast out of their bed."

Annie, typically not one to be a shoulder to cry on, had put her arm around Prithi. "You can stay here." She looked at me and I nodded, not sure why I knew we had to take in this pregnant stranger, but knowing it was the right thing to do.

"I can't pay you rent," Prithi said. "But I can cook for you."

"That's enough," I said. And the case was settled. We had a third roommate.

The meeting went on like that for another twenty minutes, although no one could top Prithi's tale of woe.

Then I brought up the thing that had been nagging at me as I listened to each of the women's stories.

"Why do you guys think we want to get married so bad? I was listening to all of you and I keep hearing the same thing: 'I go crazy because I want to get married.' What's that about?"

The room got eerily quiet because it was true, and when you bring up something that's true, people need to stop and think about it for a minute.

"I genuinely want someone to love me and spend the rest of my life with me," Lila said, twisting her pearls in between her fingers.

"My parents want me to get married. I want to make them happy," Prithi added.

"I'm afraid of being alone," Olivia said almost under her breath.

The room grew even quieter on that beat. Being alone was something we all feared.

Cameron broke the silence.

"I've watched too many seasons of *The Husband*," she offered, getting a few laughs.

The Husband was a television show that had become widely popular with women (and more than a few men; Dave, for one, was a fan) over the past decade. The show found a single guy, typically in his thirties, with a good job—like a pilot, a doctor, or the brother of someone famous—and brought in twenty-seven women, on average ten years younger and abundantly less successful than him, to catfight their way into his heart over the span of eight weeks before the Husband finally narrows it down to two ladies. They add alcohol and hilarity really ensues. Everyone awkwardly professes their love, even though in real life they've only known each other for maybe three weeks. He then whisks them both away on a terribly romantic tropical vacation where they have to pretend to get all angsty about spending the night with him, even though they know if they don't do it they're donesky. Then he dumps one and proposes marriage to the other. All in all, it has raised and lowered the bar for what we should expect from a man in the first two months of dating.

"Let's stop watching *The Husband*," I suggested. There were nods. We had made our second rule!

Rule 2: Reality dating shows are not reality. Don't drink that Kool-Aid.

That seemed like as good a note as any to end the meeting on. I suggested we all stand in a circle and hold hands. I had printed out the serenity prayer on a piece of paper and passed it around. We all said it together and then erupted again in applause. Some lingered and had coffee and donuts. Annie showed Prithi to one of the spare rooms and I clucked after everyone, pleased at how well the meeting had gone and surprised again at how much lighter and happier I felt for sitting and talking about my problems and recognizing the same problems and patterns in other women. Finally, just as I said good-bye to the last guest and told her the meeting would be held at the same place, same time the following week, the phone rang. It was Joe. He wanted to hear all the details about the day, and I was eager to divulge what a success it had been. He said he would be over in a few hours to check on Annie, and I started thinking that maybe he would think Prithi was pretty. She did have a thing for doctors after all.

I greeted Joe wearing sweats and no makeup. For some reason I didn't feel like I needed to put on airs or try to impress him. He had instantly been relegated to the category of buddy. We sipped Diet Cokes in the backyard, watching Tito, the grandson of my grandmother's longtime gardener and landscaper, Enrique, fight with a recalcitrant rosebush he was trying to relocate to the opposite side of the yard.

"So meeting number one went well, it sounds like," Joe said.

"I think so," I said eagerly. "Everyone was so excited to finally have a place to talk and share and open up. It was wonderful."

"Are you following the steps?" Joe asked.

"The steps?" I drew a blank.

"The twelve steps. That's what AA and most of the As are based on at least. There are twelve steps to conquering addiction. First you admit you have a problem and that you need something extra in your life to help restore your sanity, then step two is to surrender yourself to a higher power."

"A higher power? That sounds like some cult-talk mumbo jumbo."

"It's not like God or anything. Or it doesn't have to be. What religion are you?"

I recounted my family's failed experiment at being Presbyterian.

"OK, well, I grew up Catholic and we went to church every Sunday. After church we went to the local bar with all my Italian cousins, and starting at the ripe old age of fourteen, we were all allowed to have drinks. I always equated church with getting a little bit wasted, so the idea of embracing a higher power to get sober was kind of alien to me, too."

"So what do you do? Pray to be sober?"

"It's not about praying; it's more about accepting that something greater than your own will is helping you out. That there is something guiding you on the right path if you just let it and stop getting in its way."

"So it's more about relaxing and surrendering to the universe?"

"Exactly."

"It's like yoga! Like when you can't get into a particular pose, like that hard one where you're supposed to get your leg over your shoulder. The instructor always says to breathe and surrender, breathe and surrender."

Joe laughed. "I think it is something a little like that."

We chatted for an hour or so. I finished filling Joe in on all the women who had come to the meeting. He said he wouldn't mind stopping by to see if any of them wanted to chat one-on-one with him. I was reminded that he still had hundreds of hours of community service to fulfill before they would let him be a real-life practicing doctor again.

That night as I prepared for another bout with insomnia, I tried to think of ways to submit myself to some kind of higher power. First I got into child's pose like I do in vinyasa class, but that didn't feel right. It was too easy and my face was buried in the bed. Plus all I could think about was how my hips weren't very open, or so my yoga instructor was constantly telling me.

So I got down on my knees and prayed the way people do in old movies.

"Dear God," I started, which sounded silly. "Dear higher power" didn't sound right either. "Hey, you!" I yelled before I realized that the serenity prayer I had printed out at the meeting seemed to be the perfect thing to say here. I tried saying it three times and then crossed myself and gave a fist pump into the air.

Make a moral inventory of yourself (a.k.a. figure out what's wrong with you) and keep the hell away from Facebook

Having Prithi around became a blessing and a curse. It was a blessing because even though I did try hard, I was a terrible cook. I often forgot key ingredients like salt or eggs, making things flat and bland and inedible. It was a curse because Prithi's curries were so delicious that only two weeks after she arrived, I couldn't button my skinny jeans.

For a pregnant person Prithi was surprisingly without quirks. She never had cravings or got morning sickness and she never complained. In fact, somehow it was Annie who managed to get Prithi to give her a foot rub one night, which Prithi happily obliged. She said she used to do it for Dr. Mehti, and it made her feel good to be needed.

Prithi was our first houseguest, but she wasn't the last. On the Wednesday after the first meeting, Annie's college roommate

Melinda brought her cousin Stella over. Melinda explained that she had to get Stella out of the city due to her latest man drama. It seemed absurd to me that anyone who looked like Stella would have any kind of trouble. She had dark brown hair down to her butt, and her eyes were a bright green that didn't look like any kind of color eyes should be. Even rimmed red and swollen by tears, they were gorgeous.

Stella was speechless so we let Melinda do the talking for her.

"You don't have a TV here, do you?" were the first words out of her mouth.

"We do, but the cable is out and it's pretty old, so we just use it to watch DVDs."

"Good, good; so you don't get ABC?" This line of questioning seemed odd. Was Stella in love with a character on a television show?

"No, it comes in all fuzzy."

"OK, good," Melinda nodded. "These questions must seem so strange. I'll get to the point. Stella's boyfriend broke up with her because he didn't want to marry her."

"Commitment phobes. Common problem," Annie said, shaking her head. Participating in just one meeting of LAA seemed to be giving Annie a new glimpse into the trials and tribulations of heterosexual dating. "A lot of commitment phobes out there." Annie, who came out of the closet at age sixteen and had never lacked for female or male attention, didn't know anything about anyone not wanting to commit to her. If anything, Annie was a commitment phobe herself.

"Right, right, of course there are," Melinda said. "But the problem is Stella's boyfriend didn't just *not* want to marry her. He wants to marry someone else."

"How do you know? Does he have a fiancée already?"

"He has twenty-seven of them."

"That's ambitious," Annie said.

"And illegal, I think," I added. "Well, *maybe* not until he marries all of them. And if it isn't illegal, well, it is awfully shitty."

"You guys aren't getting it. He's the new Husband."

"As in progressive? Like the new kind of husband, the kind you can only find in Sweden, home of mandatory paternity leave?"

"No. As in the contestant on the reality show *The Husband*. He's down to the final eight. Stella stopped talking after the third tulip ceremony."

"That would drive me fucking crazy too. No wonder she's catatonic."

"She read about it in *US Weekly*," Melinda nodded. "He didn't have the balls to tell her himself."

Annie informed the ladies that we had already banned *The Husband* because of its deleterious effects on women's general self-esteem and the unrealistic expectations it set on our dating lives. Stella, obviously beaten down by her circumstances, just gave us a small smile, revealing two rows of gorgeous teeth, and trudged upstairs to join Prithi.

Then Friday night I opened the door to find a perfect butt facing me. It was just the right amount of round and high and pert and adorable. It was the kind of butt I always dreamed about having, but years of yoga had still failed to give me what nature had so obviously given this butt from birth. My eyes wandered up to a lithe frame and a mane of honey-blond hair that almost reached down to that perfect tush.

The perfection ceased when the butt's owner turned around to reveal swollen eyes, a mouth covered in powdered sugar, and a hand clutching a jelly donut like a life preserver.

"Jordana?" I asked, not believing that the flawless being I had been taking yoga from in New York for the past two years was standing on my doorstep binge eating Dunkin' Donuts and crying her eyes out. Yoga instructors are a little like models. We get these girl crushes on them, hold them up to an ideal, and never imagine that they have real people problems, the kind of problems that fleshy people who can't put their leg behind their head have. You never picture them crying or drinking or eating something with more than five hundred calories. They're simply not human—until that moment on your doorstep at two a.m. when they are.

"What are you doing here? And why so late?" Jordana and I weren't exactly friends, even though I had attended her Monday night class faithfully for twenty-four months. We had a teacher-student thing. Sometimes she moved my hip into a correct position as I blanched, trying to remember whether I properly applied deodorant that morning when her nose got uncomfortably close to my armpit. We said hello before class. I thanked her afterward with a head-bobbing, mumbling "Namaste," and that was about the extent of it.

"Amy McAlexander told me that you were holding this little

thing here for women who are going through something uncomfortable," Jordana said in Oxford-perfect English. I did happen to know that she had grown up in Leeds and was a philosophy major at the British University before seeking spiritual growth by way of the New York City yoga scene. Amy McAlexander was one of the girlfriends I regularly went to yoga with, who must have heard through the grapevine what was happening in Yardville, New Jersey.

"It's two a.m. You could have come in the morning."

"It's New Jersey. I got bloody lost. How anyone gets anywhere in this damn state with all your roundabouts and whatnot I don't know, and I was starving by the time I finally got to where I thought I should be going, but thankfully there was this delicious little boutique pastry shop open twenty-four hours."

Of course she had never stumbled across a Dunkin' Donuts chain store before. I ushered her in and realized everyone else had been awakened by the door and was gathered Brady Bunch–style lining the stairs.

There was no point in beating around the bush, even though I couldn't imagine anyone breaking up with that butt.

"Did you . . . get dumped?"

This prompted a torrent of tears, obviously not for the first time this evening.

"Do you want to talk about it?"

A nod sent snot running down her face, which prompted Stella to silently run for a tissue.

"Hey, Prithi, do you have any more of those cookies you

baked?" I yelled over my shoulder as I guided Jordana to the couch. In a lower voice I explained, "Cooking is her therapy."

"That's so smart," Jordana said, obviously uplifted by the thought of having cookies. I was worried her yoga instructor's body was going to go into sugar shock after years of healthful eating and it would be all my fault when that perfect butt ballooned up to the size of a very normal butt. As all us ladies with normal butts know, once you cross that threshold there really is no going back.

Cookies on the table and everyone seated Indian style in a circle as if we were preparing for a campfire, Jordana let loose her story.

"Well, I have been dating Paul for three years. We were living together in the West Village. We had a dog together, a rescued English bulldog named Elvis." At this point it was hard to feel sorry for Jordana since she did indeed seem to have the very perfect life I had always imagined as I glimpsed her through my downward dogs.

"He is a rolfer." Maybe not so perfect.

"Oh, honey," Prithi said. "They have over-the-counter drugs for that."

Annie nodded. "My pledge name in college was Ipecac since I used to ralph so much." She got a room full of blank stares. "You know, ipecac. It makes you throw up."

Jordana now looked horrified. "No, he practices rolfing. It's a form of bodywork and massage. It gets deep into your tissues. It is like a deep tissue massage on steroids. He rolfs."

The explanation didn't make the word any less funny, and titters continued around the circle until Jordana continued.

"One day I checked his e-mail."

A collective groan through the room.

"Snooping is public enemy number one for anyone in a relationship," I said from experience.

"As well it should be. Anyway, so I checked his e-mail and there were notifications from Nerve.com . . . so I tried to log into his Nerve.com account. And, well, it wasn't terribly hard since Elvis was his bloody password. Anyway he had been searching Nerve for dates."

"Nooooooo."

"But that's not the worst part. He was searching Nerve specifically for women who were into threesomes . . . something I told him I just wasn't into. You know, there are enough limbs flailing about in the bedroom as is; why do you need to add four more?"

I agreed with her. I had always found the intrigue over the threesome completely confounding.

"So you confronted him?"

"No, not then. I was about to when he decided to break the news to me."

"He admitted he was a dirty, lying cyber cheater?"

"No, he told me he was a dirty, lying, actual, in-real-life cheater. With a Pilates instructor, no less." Jordana said *Pilates* the same way most refined English ladies would say *poop*.

"Is that a little like defecting to the dark side?" Prithi asked.

"Yes!" Jordana practically screamed, so happy that someone understood just how big an offense her boyfriend's indiscretion with an alternative fitness instructor had been. I realized that it probably wasn't the three-way cyber peeping that had my yoga teacher in a donut-eating rage, but rather the fact that he would abandon her for what she considered a less evolved form of bodywork.

She looked sheepish for a moment.

"But now I am obsessed. I can't meditate for even thirty seconds. He is all I think about. My brain is on some kind of hamster wheel. When I walk on the street, I think every man might be Paul. Every woman looks like that Pilates-peddling bitch. When I see a fat woman who very obviously couldn't be her, I start to think about whether Paul would find this woman attractive, whether he would have a threesome with her. Every woman is my enemy, and every man has become the love of my life. I can't BLOODY turn it off."

"Welcome to the club," Prithi said.

Jordana was also homeless, and we bartered that she would stay in exchange for some morning meditation and yoga instruction we all agreed we could use. We were an inpatient and an outpatient rehab.

It was nice having the house full. It reminded me of summers when I was a kid and my grandmother invited all her own kids to come back to New Jersey, from wherever they had scattered around the country, for two weeks with their own children and sometimes the odd friend or two. At nights the adults played cards, drank wine, and stayed up late reminiscing, while all the cousins bunked on cots in the attic and bonded over the forced closeness. In this same way, I came to realize that I liked having roommates as an adult. With them came the kind of forced bonding that only happened in summer camp, where girls you never would have even spoken to at home became your lifelong best friends just because the first letter of your last name got you placed in the same cabin, and then you all got your first periods together.

I ended up sharing the master bedroom with Katrina. She was a woman I never could have imagined making my girlfriend when she arrived with her six pieces of matching Louis Vuitton luggage and a very small terrier named Nahla.

"I'm here for the love retreat," she announced imperiously when Annie opened the door. Katrina's chin was cocked just an inch above where most of us let it hang from our heads, her eyes hidden behind giant Marc Jacobs sunglasses.

"Retreat?" Annie asked. "We're doing something called Love Addicts Anonymous."

"Don't be silly. *Retreat* is such a better marketing buzzword. All the real rehabs are retreats, breaks, just like all overdoses involve being hospitalized for 'exhaustion.' *Love retreat* has a much better ring to it anyway, don't you think?"

I wasn't there but I can imagine Annie wanting to slam the door in the face of Katrina (whom she immediately nicknamed Princess Katrina in her head, a moniker that we eventually shortened to Princess). But then Katrina did something only a princess (a true princess like Kate Middleton, not a faux princess like one of those Italian or Danish princesses who wear pantyhose with open-toed sandals and run away with their jockeys) could do—she won Annie over.

"I love your tattoo," she said, admiring the labyrinth Annie did not remember inking on her upper right arm after a trip to Mexico.

Katrina went on, "I'm very into Mayan culture. Anyway, I walked the labyrinth the entire time I was doing a yoga retreat down in Tulum and it was the best meditation I have ever done. I can't sit and meditate, so walking and meditating was simply perfect for me. The labyrinth looks like it fits you though. You look like the kind of person who always has to be on the move. Like a strong person who knows exactly what she wants in life."

At that, Princess reached out and enveloped Annie, who had no idea what the tattoo meant, just that she woke up on spring break in Tijuana with a permanent reminder of a gorgeous Mexican tattoo artist named Maria permanently on her body, in a bear hug.

"Thank you so much for having me," Katrina declared, walking right past Annie into the living room, up the stairs, and into my room, where she plopped all six of the Louis Vuitton bags on the spare bed we had just dragged up from the basement and sat Indian style filing her nails, waiting for me to wake up.

Princess was terrifyingly put together on the outside and commanded an air of respect. More than that, she genuinely liked almost everyone she met and wanted to hug them and shower them with compliments and find ways to make their lives better, often through crystals, herbs, or skin care advice.

Her full-time job was a singular quest for self-improvement fueled by a hearty trust fund. She didn't have to work, since her father was the famed engineer who invented the thing that makes SUVs beep when you're about to back into something. Princess was therefore free to spend her days seeking various spiritual and physical guidance strategies, which made her a walking self-help encyclopedia. She had instructors for and/ or personal certifications in everything from crystal healing, herbology, the Alexander technique, psychic powers, acupuncture, acupressure, Thai massage, Pilates, yoga, rolfing!, macrotherapy, hydrotherapy, psychotherapy, and a little bit of voodoo. She had traveled the globe, hopping from one retreat to the next, looking to find herself.

Like the other ladies I had met in LAA, Princess was a great-looking girl. Compact and smaller than her personality made her appear, she had near-black hair long enough for her to sit on and an angular face. She dressed perfectly for her curvy body type, wearing clothes that accentuated exactly what needed accentuating and hid any flaws.

Princess hadn't recently been dumped. But her crystal healer told her that she needed to break a recurring habit of hers that kept leading to heartbreak and would prevent her from ever finding true love. She kept dating gay men. Most of the time she didn't know they were gay when she started dating them. She just knew they were incredibly well dressed, neat, and quick to compliment her Jil Sander mules, loved to accompany her to the theater, and showered her with affection.

Always came the day when they sat her down to tell her they loved her, couldn't get enough of her. They needed to still be with her almost every second of every day, but they wanted to sleep with men. It happened thirteen times. She confided in her crystal healer, whose name is actually Crystal, that the seventh one didn't quite sit her down to have the talk; instead she came home to find him dressed in full drag in her very best Zac Posen evening gown, all her Fred Leighton jewels, and a long brown wig, wearing a Harry Winston tiara on his head. She thought she was looking into a mirror. He was dressing in drag as her. Of course, being Princess and able to skillfully manage any situation, she told him she was flattered and that she was impressed with his technique of makeup mastery, but he did need to go easier on the blush and a little higher on the cheekbones next time. She broke it to him that they could no longer be together, but she still goes to see his show every Thursday in the West Village. It's called "Katrina, Katrina."

Her psychotherapist said all these men had mommy issues and Katrina fulfilled the role of the perfectly appointed and loving mother none of them had ever had. Her acting teacher told her she was their Judy Garland, which didn't make a whole lot of sense to me because I remember reading somewhere that Judy Garland wasn't a very excellent mother. She did create Liza Minnelli after all.

It was Crystal who had heard from her Chinese herb expert that there was a love retreat going on in New Jersey and she thought maybe Katrina could sort her problems outside of the city. So Princess had tracked us down and now she was ready to be rehabbed, or retreated—as the posh would call it.

Princess had an entire suitcase full of the most amazing bath products you've ever seen and a second just with vitamins and herbs meant to treat any sort of anxious disorder. She went straight to work creating a mulberry tea to cure my insomnia, which made me sleep like a baby for the first time in months. Like Annie before me I fell in love with Princess before I could think about hating her.

LAA had become a mismatched family, still completed by our "outpatients" who commuted in on Sundays.

What did we all have in common? Sure, we had been mistreated by men, but the big thing was that we had all *allowed* ourselves to be mistreated by men (big thanks to Joe for that revelation). So the point of our group meetings was to help one another break that cycle. Not only did we need to admit that we had a problem and talk about that problem, but we also had to stop doing the things that contributed to the problems in the first place.

That Sunday we sat in the circle and each woman reviewed her progress.

"My name is Prithi, and I am a love addict," Prithi started off her monologue, one hand on her lower back and the other gesticulating her words. "I'm feeling better this week. But I slipped. I sent the doctor eleven text messages. He responded to one. It was very short and cold and then I cried for about five hours. I took an Instagram of the flowers that Sophie brought home the other day and I posted them on my Facebook wall with a caption that said, 'Oh, you shouldn't have,' to try to make him jealous."

Everyone nodded gravely, not making any judgments.

"I think I will be stronger this week," Prithi said with conviction. Applause.

"I'm Cameron, and I'm a love addict. I met a guy this week. I've seen him around for a while. I think he lives in my neighborhood because he is always at my Trader Joe's and this time we happened to be reaching for the same prepackaged Tandoori Butter Chicken. We literally touched it at the same time. We laughed. He asked me if I wanted to get a drink. Then I did what I always do. Every time I meet a man who might be suitable for a long-term relationship I start to play out the whole damn thing in my head. We would always have that tandoori chicken as an inside joke. It would be our code phrase for when we wanted to cut out early from some terrible dinner with my work friends."

I did the same thing when I illustrated a meet-cute from the beginning of a relationship.

"He was a little tan, which I took to mean he liked the beach. We could spend summer weekends at my parents' place in Avalon. This all happened in the space of thirty seconds. We had the drink. That drink turned into another drink. We went back to my place and fooled around a little before I told him I had an early meeting. He texted me two days later to say he had a good time. Then I texted him to see if he wanted to come to my cousin's wedding on Friday."

The only sound was the soft click of jaws dropping.

"Since I had imagined our entire damn relationship in my head, it seemed like the right thing to do."

"And?" I asked.

"I haven't heard anything from him."

Erin was seventeen going on thirty, just like most high school girls I know. An adolescence spent with *Sex and the City* re-runs, along with the latest episodes of *Teen Mom* and *Jersey Shore*, made the pretty young blonde wise beyond her years. I nervously wondered whether we needed parental permission to have someone under eighteen come to the meetings, but her stories were so juicy that I didn't have it in me to ask. I used to babysit her, so that would have to do.

A senior in high school, Erin was an über-overachiever. She played on three varsity sports teams, was student council president, and proudly joined the yearbook staff. She was also a less-than-proud recent dumpee.

"Last week they let me start writing the captions for yearbook photos," Erin said, after telling us all about how her boyfriend of three years unceremoniously gave her the boot. "I found a picture of him getting his blood drawn at the school blood drive. I added the caption, 'Just a little prick.'"

The room roared with laughter, tinged with just a hint of jealousy, at how clever Erin was for someone who was still too young to vote or drink vodka.

Kirsten, a forty-two-year-old, very Caucasian, chain-smoking florist who insisted on gesticulating with an electronic cigarette, made me nervous for entirely different reasons. I was a little concerned she might be arrested.

"I called up the mom of this twenty-two-year-old gangsta wannabe whom I caught back with his baby mama last week," she said, making what may have been a gang symbol out of her index and middle fingers and the plastic cigarette. "So I called up *his* mama and told her that he had given me AIDS."

Princess gasped. "You have AIDS? Like Magic Johnson?"

Kirsten just laughed. "No, bitch. I just told his mom that."

"That might be worse," I heard Annie mutter under her breath.

Liz was a friend of my grandmother's from her bridge club. She had fiery red hair, and even though it was clearly created by Clairol and not the good Lord, that didn't stop her from once telling me that the carpet did indeed match the drapes. I was seven years old at the time.

"I am Liz, and I am a love addict!" she announced with a flourish. Like Eleanor, Liz seemed to have a new gentleman caller every week. This week, she had found out that Adam, who was a hot commodity on the senior market because he still had his own teeth, was trying to hook up with other women online.

"I made a fake Facebook profile and friended him. He immediately sent me a private message asking to meet me. What a slimeball!"

The room nodded in agreement.

"When I was the one who showed up at the restaurant, the look on his face was priceless. At first he didn't realize he had been busted. He asked if I was there with someone. He had the nerve to think that I was cheating on *him*! A minute later, he figured it out. I tossed my Skinnygirl margarita in his face and I got outta there."

Liz finished with three snaps.

Lila had brought along a printout of an e-mail she received from the guy she was seeing. They had gone home together for the first time and he hadn't been able to perform. It was a secret relief because Lila really wasn't that into him to begin with and she thought that gave her a good opportunity to call it quits.

Hey Lila,

I lied to you. On Saturday you asked me if you were the first person I'd been with since my breakup, and I said yes. Actually, I'd had an unexpected one-night stand just the night before with a friend of a friend who was passing through NYC. I don't feel I owed you any fidelity. But I felt weird telling you about it right then and I'm rusty with the complexities of casual dating, so I panicked and fibbed. (Also, I think I was seizing on the "first time" thing as an excuse for my failure to launch. The actual excuse is that I'd been up the whole night before having sex. Plus the drinking.)

Given the circumstances, I'm telling you now.

I like spending time with you. I'd be happy to spend more

time with you. I'd enjoy another chance to get comfortable
with you in bed and rock your world. But if this is the end of
the road, I have zero regrets.

Peace,
Max

"So what should I do?" Lila asked, genuinely bewildered.

Annie was the first to reply, probably because she was usually on the sending end of such missives.

"You never talk to him again. He's gross. That e-mail is fucked up."

Lila slumped in her chair.

"I thought it was sweet."

That was another problem we were all having. We didn't know what good communication with men was even like anymore. They threw us the tiniest of slivers of bones, like, "I like spending time with you," and we forget that a paragraph earlier they told us they lied to us about having sex with someone else the night before our date.

It went on like that as every woman stood up around the room.

"I texted nine times."

"I checked his e-mail again."

"I Facebook stalked his new girlfriend."

"I followed his every move on Instagram and then started going to the same coffee shop in the morning."

That began a twenty-minute discussion of what was more

dangerous when it came to cyber stalking, Facebook or Instagram. Facebook provided more depth for the serious stalker, more photos, a deeper dive into whom they were spending time with, but Instagram gave an immediacy that is poisonous for a woman hanging by a thread.

"I drove by his house four times."

"I told a mutual friend he had the clap."

"I created a fake e-mail account to e-mail my ex, claiming my name was Marianne Faithfull, but I wasn't *the* Marianne Faithfull."

"I was hammered and out, and Hot Bobby [a guy Olivia had gone on two and a half dates with] was home and sober. So obviously I go over there and we hook up. He had a teeny tiny room with a modular closet with his television on top. I started asking him if he would consider me his girlfriend. He wouldn't answer. So I got up butt-ass naked and for whatever reason started walking on top of the bed toward the door like I was leaving. Hot Bobby was, like, grabbing at my foot and I was kicking and trying to avoid him. I started to fall forward and reached for one of the shelves to steady me. I tore down Hot Bobby's closet, television and all. Do you think he will text me again?"

We shook our heads.

Rule 3: Stop the drunk booty call. It is never, ever attractive.

"I'll miss hearing about Hot Bobby," Lila said.

Jordana cocked her head to one side. "Hot Bobby's Closet

sounds a bit like a home decorating show hosted by a scrumptious homosexual on the Bravo network."

"Mmmmm. Or an indie punk band fronted by Jared Leto," I said.

We spent the next five minutes in a sidebar talking about our collective tween crushes on Jordan Catalano and the way he just leaned on things.

As each woman divulged her dirty little secret for the week, you could see her visibly relax, like a weight had been removed from her shoulders. It felt nice to be able to tell people our secret crazy. It felt much better than telling our "noncrazy" friends, who we knew in our heart of hearts would say, "Yes, of course that makes sense," before getting on the phone with someone else to recount how very sad they believed us to be.

Since I still felt a little in charge of the group, I suggested we brainstorm some more rules to break these patterns.

"No more social media," Lila said. "Facebook and Twitter and Pinterest are ruining my life."

"Pinterest?" Princess asked with curiosity. "I thought that one was just for posting pictures of pretty food, puppies, and Robert Pattinson with his shirt off."

"Oh, it is," Lila said. "But the problem is that I can access my ex's new girlfriend's Pinterest page. I tried to copy her recipe for crème brûlée cupcakes yesterday, and I ordered one of the throw cushions that she embroiders with horrible inspirational phrases. It says 'hang in there.'"

"It's good advice," I said sympathetically. "You are hanging in there."

"I don't want to hang in there with her goddamned pillow!" Lila, who was normally quite composed, erupted. She quickly got ahold of herself. "Anyway, I think the ability to peek in on ex-boyfriends and their new girlfriends' lives is dangerous."

Cameron chimed in. "Not just exes, but new or potential boyfriends. I knew everything about Tandoori Chicken Guy ten minutes after our date."

Eyebrows raised at Cam's use of the word *date*.

"Was it really a date?" Annie asked.

"Ughhhh. I think everything is a date. I was already figuring out how our lives fit together based on his Facebook pictures."

They had hit the nail on the head. Social media didn't create our neuroses or unhealthy obsessions. Let's face it; women have been driving themselves crazy over men since Adam taunted Eve about how she shouldn't eat the apple because the apple would make her chubby. Eve ate the damn thing out of spite and became man's scapegoat number one for all eternity.

Still, social media did allow our too, too complex lady brains to go into hyperdrive, facilitating the cycle of addiction to romantic love.

"No more social media," I said with conviction. "Let's just spend some time offline and see how that works out for us."

Everyone nodded in agreement.

We had our fourth rule!

Rule 4: Never mix social media and relationships, until he puts a ring on it . . . then maybe.

Then I proposed an activity that Joe had suggested to help us figure out our behavior patterns. We needed to create a moral inventory. It was the fourth of the proper twelve steps.

"What's a moral inventory?" Jordana asked.

"I've done that one before," Katrina said, sitting up with excitement after lying prone on the floor with two quartz crystals balanced precariously on her cheekbones to alleviate tension in her gallbladder. "I did it when I went to a silent retreat in Bern. It's where you make a list of all the things you do that keep you from achieving your best self."

"That one sounds fun," Jordana said, the room nodding in agreement.

It was a nice simple step to begin with. How hard could it be to write down what was wrong with you? It seemed much harder to write down all the things that were right, and we were already on such a roll after the weekly progress reports. I grabbed a stack of sketch pads that I used to sketch out ideas for work and a handful of pencils, figuring people would want to erase as they went along. I told everyone we would devote fifteen minutes to making our lists and then reconvene to read them and talk about them.

Five minutes in I realized this was much harder than it seemed. What did I do wrong in my relationships that made them all end badly? Of course, all relationships end badly until, hopefully, the one that never ends at all. What had I particularly done with Eric? Right off the bat I think that I might have come on too strong. Cameron and I definitely had that in common. Only two months into our relationship I had three glasses of wine and babbled "I love you" as we were having sex. Eric ignored me. The next morning I defensively brought it up.

"You know, when I said I loved you last night, I didn't mean it. Everyone says things like that during sex."

"I know," he said without batting an eye over the Sports section of the *New York Times*.

"But what did you think when I said it?" I pushed.

"I thought, man, I'm about to come." He smiled and tweaked my boob, a habit that hurt more than tickled but that I had come to find endearing.

"Did you think 'I love you too'?" I wasn't prepared to let it go.

"I thought I was about to come," he said, pulling me into his lap and making that statement a reality then and there.

I kept on like that, slipping "accidental" "love you"s into conversations where I could claim deniability later and then bickering over them in the morning, until finally one day he relented and submitted to a "love ya too" (emphasis strongly on the *ya*, as if by leaving off two letters the entire meaning of the phrase could be inexorably altered), after which point I proceeded to tack on an "I love you" to every phone conversation and before we parted, until it became pretty commonplace and he simply accepted that it was something we were now saying and doing. After a while I suppose I had forgotten how it all started and come to believe that he was a willing participant in the lovefest. And after that I simply shifted the narrative of how we fell in love in my head.

I wrote down "needy" on my list followed by "pushy." And then added "too quick to fall in love." Then I had a breakthrough. This was something I did with all my boyfriends leading up to Eric too. Eric was no anomaly.

It went all the way back to Michael Macintyre in high school. I made a binder of what our wedding would look like and gave it to him before he went off to college a year before me. That was before cell phones, but even I knew the reason he never answered the phone in his dorm.

I was a love pusher. I just wanted my boyfriends to like me so much that I never really considered whether I liked them. It just felt good to make someone like me.

Surprised to find fifteen minutes up and just three things on my list, I reconvened the group.

"I'll go first." I broke the ice. "I'm a needy love pusher. I make people tell me they love me before they've ever had a chance to fall in love with me." This was met with nods of approval.

"That's all?" Katrina said.

"It was only fifteen minutes, and I think that is actually quite a big revelation for me. I don't think I ever realized it was something I did until just now. In my head I genuinely thought all 'I love you's came organically and that love just happened to me through a series of madcap moments the way it does in Reese Witherspoon movies, but if you look back through my catalog of boyfriends the 'love issue' always came up under duress instigated by me."

And that wasn't all of it. "Since it was said under duress, I made them all feel trapped and eventually they grew to completely despise me.

"The bigger problem," I admitted, "is I don't know if I actually loved them or just wanted to be in love." I was starting to realize that there was a big difference. Everyone clapped, and Prithi put her arm around me when I sat down.

Katrina looked like she approved before she stood in front of the group with two pages of her flaws.

I crossed my arms. It wasn't quite fair that she was so adept at this listicling since she had done this before and on a silent retreat no less, where she probably had days of peace and quiet and Swedish massage to come up with all her moral failings.

Stella wrote down her moral failings, and Melinda, who was coming weekly as her translator, read them aloud.

"I turn into a chameleon. I pretend to like what they like. If they like the Beatles, then I like the Beatles, even though I think 'Here Comes the Sun' is one of the worst songs ever written. If they like running, I pretend to like running. I act like I like sashimi when really I only like raw fish in rolls. I think that by becoming more like them they will like me."

We all nodded. Everyone did at least a little bit of that. While dating a Colombian in college I pretended to be completely into the fútbol (I even pronounced it like I imagined Gisele would: the Foooootbowl), when I couldn't name a single position in the fútbol (soccer, damnit) besides the goalie.

Cameron raised her hand.

"I envy people in relationships." We looked at her quizzically. Of course we all envied people in relationships. Somehow relationships became the be-all and end-all of what women strive for in their twenties and thirties. Even as we pretend we're striving for something else, like a great career or that perfect ass or self-actualization through lots of yoga and meditation, we still sneak a peek at the left ring finger of every man we meet to see if he is worth spending our time talking to. We still hope and pray that every man we encounter is going to be the one who sweeps us off our feet and declares our dating days dead in the water.

But Cameron had more to say. "I kind of hate them. And I don't want to hate them, especially my friends. I want to look at my friends who are in relationships and be totally happy for them because they've achieved something that I want. If a friend of mine runs a marathon or climbs a mountain, I am proud of them. If they get a man to ask them to move in with them, I don't want to talk to them for weeks. And it makes me feel like a bad person. It makes me feel even worse, but somehow I can't stop it."

I got her. To some extent we all hate our married or long-term coupled friends. I think that's why Bridget Jones decided to refer to them as the "smug marrieds," because what else could we say about them? For the most part, save for a few couples that I don't think ever should have gotten together (he's gay, she's a mensch), my married friends are quite happy. They have something I want, but maybe I should have just been happy that what I wanted was out there and possible instead of feeling awful when one of my friends' husbands stroked his wife's back or texted her something funny, just because he happened to be thinking about her during our brunch date on a Saturday.

Once everyone had their turn and felt properly unburdened of what had turned into a multitude of issues, the room was decidedly blue. Admitting what is wrong with you is not a fun game and while LAA wasn't supposed to be a bed of roses, we were supposed to leave feeling better about ourselves. It was also hard to accept that what we were lonely for was actually someone we hadn't met yet. We didn't so much miss all the jerks we were leaving behind as we were terrified of not finding the one that was right for us.

The camp counselor in me (TRUTH: I only survived one summer of camp counseloring due to my aversion to bugs, an extreme allergy to poison ivy, and Annie not being invited back after canoeing to the boys' side of camp to buy some bootleg tequila) came out.

"This is a good thing, ladies," I blurted out with a tad too much contrived enthusiasm. "We don't have to feel like shit because of what we've done in the past. The point of this exercise is to own our faults and try not to repeat them. I have an idea if everyone can stay just a little bit longer."

Everyone agreed they had nowhere better to be on a Sunday night. I left them to their devices while I scoured the garage for Eleanor's personal guilty pleasure—hoping that no one had moved it since the funeral.

It ended up being pretty easy to find. Covered by a sheet in the far back corner of the car port was a karaoke machine complete with two microphones. It took me only a few minutes to set it up on the television in the basement, thanks to Eleanor's detailed cursive instructions left for her nurses on how to make the thing work. I remembered that when she was on her last legs, she demanded to karaoke with her support staff on Sunday nights, singing mainly show tune staples. Tito, Eleanor always said, did a wonderful baritone "Surrey with the Fringe on Top."

My grandmother was partial to Pat Benatar.

I called everyone to the basement.

"Here's what we're going to do. Everyone pick a song that you think represents your worst moral failing and sing it."

There was a groan, but I decided to translate it as a groan of delight. Of course I could have been deluding myself. Maybe I was also a karaoke pusher. But if I was, I didn't care. I couldn't imagine how anyone wouldn't be happier after a few rounds of karaoke.

Katrina went first, choosing Aretha Franklin's "Respect," since high on her list was the fact that she didn't think she respected herself enough to search for a man who loved her for the right reasons. Stella hummed along to Sinéad O'Connor's "Nothing Compares 2 U," since her biggest failing, conveyed to us through a series of notes, was that she was unable to appreciate herself as much as the boyfriends she always put on a pedestal. Prithi sang "Papa Don't Preach," natch.

I went through the list of thousands of songs stored in the machine until I came up with the perfect song for my personal moral inventory.

I was so into "I Would Do Anything for Love" that it wasn't

until I was to hell and back about four times (who knew the abridged version of the song was seven minutes!) before I realized that Joe had crashed our meeting and was standing on the stairs holding his lighter aloft in the air and waving it back and forth. I blushed but finished the last two and a half minutes, totally breathless, to cheers and applause, delighted that I had jarred the room out of its self-inflicted depression. Two hours later a very happy crew dispersed in a haze of melodic humming, with an extra bob in their steps.

Joe stuck around to help clean and chatted with Annie about her upcoming court appearance where she had to chat with the judge about her progress in therapy.

"Karaoke, huh?" he said when we were momentarily alone in the kitchen.

"We did a moral inventory of our flaws and everyone was so bummed that I had to do something to brighten the mood," I explained. "Karaoke makes everyone happy."

"Not if you can't carry a tune," he said.

"Especially if you can't carry a tune."

"Not me. I hate doing anything I am bad at. I'm awful at just letting go if I know I can't do things perfectly. I'm actually awful at letting go altogether except when I drink."

"Is that why you drink?"

"I think that alcoholics and addicts are predisposed to their drug of choice but, yeah, I think I drank when I wanted to loosen up and that it got out of control." Joe seemed ready to shift the topic away from him when he asked, "What was on your moral inventory?"

I paused before letting it spill.

"I'm a love pusher. I make men tell me they love me before they're ready and then when they don't end up actually loving me, I am all the more hurt because we were supposed to be in love. Does that make any sense at all?"

"Have you ever watched a pelican eat?" Joe asked.

"Way to change the subject, but, OK, I'll bite. No, I don't think I have ever watched a pelican do anything. So eat, pelican, no."

"Well, pelicans eat fish and they fly over the ocean watching the water until they see the perfect fish that they want for their dinner. If you watch them when they make their decision, it looks like they're falling out of the sky. They literally drop into the ocean like dead weight and plummet headfirst into the water. But they always get their fish."

"Always?"

"Ninety-eight percent of the time."

"Wow."

"It's a little like falling in love. They see what they want. They throw caution to the wind and they go for it. They literally fall head over heels from the sky."

"But they always know they're going to get their fish."

"That's why I wouldn't want to be a pelican," Joe said.

"That doesn't make any sense."

"They know things will work out every single time they let themselves go. It's got to get boring after a while. There's no challenge in it after the first ten times. I would rather fall and miss that fish a dozen times and then finally catch the right one. The fattest, juiciest, fishiest of the fish. Because then I would feel like I really deserved that fish. Like I worked for it."

"Why do you know so much about pelicans? Were you a middle-school science teacher in a past life?"

Joe laughed. "I was a nerd. A serious nerd all through high school. I had acne and glasses and was shy as hell, so I watched a lot of the History and Discovery Channels."

"Better than Dungeons and Dragons."

"I did that, too. I also built my own computers."

"So back to the pelicans. I don't get it."

"You dove after every fish, Sophie. You wanted all the fish to be a great catch and since not every fish can be a great catch, you tried to turn the bad catches into good catches by convincing yourself that the two of you were in love. The pelicans may catch every fish every time, but some of those fish are rotten or bony or just swallowed a syringe and now they have fish AIDS. If you just wait, then one of these days that fat, juicy fish will be right under you waiting for you to fall for it."

"And then I'll eat it?"

"It isn't a perfect metaphor."

For the first time since the AA meeting I was nervous around Joe. He seemed like such a good fish.

But then I realized, as per usual, I was likely getting ahead of myself.

Admit to yourself and someone else all the crazy shit you have done

"I'm Cameron, and I'm a love addict. This week I booty texted three ex-boyfriends."

Cameron had gone off the deep end after running into Vegan Biter with his new fiancée. I pointed out that the silver lining of that particular run-in is that there is indeed someone for everyone.

To save time, Cameron texted all three at once.

I miss you. Come over.

Well, all three came over. In fact, they all met in the elevator and drunkenly chatted about the proximity of a very delicious underground hot dog shop around the corner that fried their hot dogs before wrapping them in bacon and frying them again before covering them in both chili and cheese. A sad truth is that at three in the morning many a man will choose greasy food over sex that he likely can't see through to completion. So they all set off together, and Cameron was left alone in her apartment. She was given the information from Maxem, her faithful doorman, whom she had also once tried to make out with after seeing her college boyfriend pushing a baby stroller down the street.

"Why did I let Vegan Biter upset me so much?" Cameron wailed. "Why did I care? I didn't like him when he bit me, but when I thought I couldn't have him anymore because he belonged to someone else, all of a sudden I can't get him out of my damn head."

We all admitted to having a hamster wheel in our head.

"I think I do it because I watched my parents and their really unhappy marriage," Cameron volunteered. "In the back of my mind, that seems normal, because I don't really have positive role models for how love should be. I think drama equals love so I just chase the drama instead of trying to find someone who can make me really happy."

"Low self-esteem," Katrina chimed in, adding the caveat, "I've been asked this before."

"Bloody romantic comedies," Jordana blurted out. "I mean, all they do is tell us that true love is simply one hilarious misunderstanding away and once that hilarious misunderstanding is overcome, then you will live happily ever after. It is bullshit. I didn't find a hilarious misunderstanding in my boyfriend's e-mail. I found a fucking pervert! There is no misunderstanding that. But if this were a romantic comedy, those e-mails would all be part of an elaborate hoax he was staging for a buddy for his stag night. Did that thought run through my mind? OF COURSE IT DID. That is why these romantic comedies are ruining our lives."

Stella applauded and snapped her fingers.

We all agreed. Romantic comedies had in some way contributed to all of us obsessing over the idea of romantic love. But how could we break that cycle right now? We really had no choice but to do what we did next. In order to debunk their lies, we had to expose ourselves to them—all of them.

And so the next twenty-four hours straight were spent watching every romantic comedy we could order up on Netflix. We laughed and groaned and discussed (ad nauseum) why these movies were absolutely nothing like real life.

This was aversion therapy. Anytime one of us got too into one scene or cried a little too much, someone would pinch her— hard enough to leave a mark.

Along the way we made a list debunking all the lies that romantic comedies have told us—a kind of treatise or "mission statement" (fuck you, *Jerry Maguire*, for trying to have us at hello) of what we should believe to replace what decades of chick flicks from *When Harry Met Sally* to *Letters to Juliet* had programmed into our brains.

1. **The nerdy guy should not always get the girl.**
   Nerd is the new douche. The chubby, less attractive alternative to the macho dick is also likely a dick. Nerds have an ax to grind and once they finally land a chick they don't always treat her like a princess. Instead they take out years

of their pent-up rejection anxiety on the relationship. And today's nerd isn't an underdog. They're likely a tech millionaire. You know what Duckie Dale is doing right now? Coding for Facebook and shitting gold bricks.

2. Your best friend is not your soul mate.

Damn *My Best Friend's Wedding* and *When Harry Met Sally*. This fantasy is the most dangerous of all the lies romantic comedies tell you because it seems so plausible. Yes, your male best friend, the one who has nursed you through countless breakups with margaritas and karaoke, who already sleeps in your bed when he spends the night (but nothing ever happens, natch), who has seen you puke, fart, and burp, *and* has touched your legs when they weren't shaved, is definitely the man you should spend the rest of your life with. The problem with this scenario is that your best friend . . . is gay.

3. The biggest cad in the world does not want marriage and children, even if you manage to catch him at the right time.

There is not a magical right time. What he wants is to continue being a cad. Forever. And not even overcoming that hilarious misunderstanding is going to fix that.

4. The cool, really attractive, popular guy isn't actually very sensitive and he does not secretly love you.

How do you know he is actually a douche? He isn't even

112

nice to his popular, really attractive girlfriend. In fact, he would sell her to a nerd for something he could find on Google.

5. There is no such thing as a soul mate.

There isn't a "one." There are probably lots of ones and mates and people who will touch our souls, but looking for *the one* is crazy.

6. And finally, love is not one hilarious misunderstanding away.

True love will not happen after you butt heads for almost a year before he tells you that all his glowering stares were directed at your womanizing boss and not you before he reads your diary and goes to buy you a new one because he gets that you were just being quirky when you wrote a bunch of nasty things about him. It won't happen after he decides to get revenge on you when you have amnesia by pretending you are his wife even though you are a really rich heiress with a yacht and a slutty husband, and it certainly won't happen after he picks you up on Hollywood Boulevard and then tells his chubby lawyer you are a hooker, forcing you to leave him even though it is true that you are indeed a hooker. We don't live in an episode of *Three's Company.*

We printed up these dictums and we decided to read them at the opening of our meetings. It was our version of the serenity prayer to ensure there would be no more hilarious misunder-standings. And then we added a new rule.

Rule 5: Thou shalt not believe the myths of the romantic comedy. Thou may only indulge for the snappy dialogue.

The Sunday after our emotional hara-kiri via John Hughes and Nora Ephron, we were again cross-legged on the floor like a kindergarten class alert after nap time. We had a guest speaker. Suze Heart stood in front of us, her platinum-blond hair so bright it practically reflected the light back at us or at least bounced it down to her shiny powder-blue tracksuit.

Within a minute of silence she had managed to elevator eye every one of us from our sneakers to the crowns of our heads.

Another division of my publishing house was publishing a self-help book by the self-made love coach Suze. Called *Tough Love: Take It or Be Sad and Lonely Forever*, it was poised to enter the bestseller list at number three just like Suze's past books, *You're a Whiner* and *Get the Hell Out of My Bed*.

During her last book tour, Suze had come off too strong and actually made two men in the audience of an author talk and book signing cry by telling them their mothers had ruined them for all other women. Since then she had been working to soften her image, so Megan thought it would be helpful to give her some practice by sending her out to New Jersey for the day to speak to our motley crew.

"How many of you are obsessive dialers?" Suze asked us without introducing herself or asking us anything about ourselves.

Five hands rose before Suze clarified, defining obsessive dialing as calling more than twice in an hour after getting an answering machine. Four more hands went up.

"What's the point?" Suze yelled. "Do you think it's 1987 and you're dialing a rotary phone that doesn't have caller ID and maybe just maybe they missed a call and have no way of knowing that you called or who called them? They know. It's on their phone and when you're through it ends up being on their phone twenty times. And you know what they're doing as they hit the ignore button on their phones? They're showing their friends the nineteenth call from this crazy-ass girl who will still sleep with them if they just answer their phone on call twenty and then say something slightly nice to her."

The truth was totally harsh.

Suze's eyes rested on Prithi for just a moment as she switched gears. "Pull the goalie?"

Prithi ducked her head and moved her arms protectively around her nearly nine-month belly. Suze walked over and chucked her under the chin the way my grandfather used to do.

"Don't you be ashamed, little lady, pulled the goalie twice myself. Have two beautiful kids. Wouldn't change a thing. It's all about what we learn from what we do and how we make ourselves a better person each time." Suze strode back to the front

115

of the room. "I didn't learn my lesson that first time and I did it again and then I learned my lesson. Nothing wrong with that since the lesson got learned. Here's what we need to do, ladies. We need to live our lives in a spiral, a spiral all moving toward AWESOME YOU."

Suze drew a swirly shape on the blackboard behind her and a stick figure in the middle with a big round circle at its midsection that we just assumed was a pregnant stick Prithi.

"Right now you're probably in a cycle, and that's no good because a cycle goes around and around doing the same thing over and over again."

She repeated her earlier question.

"How many of you are obsessive dialers?"

All hands in the room shot in the air.

"It's a funny thing, obsessively dialing these men who treat us like shit, who don't call us. Who tell us they don't want to be with us. It's funny because who the hell uses the phone anymore? None of you, right? I'll bet you Facebook your mom to say hi and how are you doing, but call, no one calls anyone. You even text your friends when you get a promotion at work. Except you call that one douchebag who doesn't want you to call him. That's why it's funny."

Suze picked up a piece of chalk and wrote in giant pink letters on the chalkboard—FAF. "You are going to FAF. Fone A Friend. That's right. We never call our friends when we want to chat about the good shit, do we? Well, we will now. You pick a designated friend, one who can put up with your loads of BS once in a while, and you name that friend the nasty son of a bitch in your phone. When you want to make seventeen phone calls in the span of an hour to say you miiiiiissss him, you call your goddamned friend. Cycle one. BROKEN."

When Suze said "Broken," she spiked the chalk on the floor like it was a football and it shattered into a hundred shards. Now I understood why she requested we supply her with six boxes of chalk.

It went on like that for about an hour and a half and we went though two more boxes of chalk before Suze said she was hungry just as the doorbell rang. A pimply-faced teen balanced four pepperoni pizzas on his arms.

"How many pepperoni on each of those pizzas, Mikey?" Suze called from the living room without even looking out the door to see who it was.

"Twenty-two, Suze," Mikey replied like his life depended on it. I tried to slip him some cash, but he just shook his head and muttered, "Already paid for," before scurrying back to his Chevy Impala with a Crazy Eddie's Pepperoni Palace sign balanced on the top. When the hell did Suze order pizza? How did she know where to call, and what was up with the twenty-two pieces of pepperoni? I didn't even want to know the answers to these questions. I was a little in love with this woman who seemed to have complete control over every aspect of her life.

Suze was full of stories and metaphors, half of them involving sports, the other half involving wild animals. Joe, with his penchant for the Discovery Channel, would have loved her, except Joe had to do some work at the hospital today and wasn't able to be there.

One story she told stuck with me.

She began each of her stories with "Did you hear about . . ." So "Did you hear about the golfer who couldn't drive to save his life but was an ace on the putting green?" "Did you hear about the baboons who let the males impregnate them and then raise their baby baboons in female-centric tribes, forcing the men to wander the savannah alone looking for their next fertile female?"

Then, "Did you hear about the loneliest whale in the world?" This is the one that got me. Scientists tracked the loneliest whale for years. She didn't have any friends. She didn't have a family, tribe, pack, or gang. She never had a lover. Why? Her voice was unlike any other baleen whale. The rest of the whales sing at a level between 12 and 25 hertz. She sang at 52 hertz. None of the other whales could hear her. All her desperate calls to communicate went unanswered.

I imagined that massive whale floating alone and singing her song to her fellow whales and none of them hearing her. She didn't know she was different. She just knew she was always alone.

Of course, the moral of the story (all Suze's stories had morals) was that if we weren't communicating with men on the same level, then they couldn't hear us and we were bound to be alone. If in our heads we were picturing our wedding day on our first date—or in Cameron's case picturing family beach vacations in

Avalon—and proceeding with that path in our mind but never communicating what we wanted, it was no wonder these guys turned tail and ran. Our songs were being sung at a frequency out of their range so that when they finally caught a smidgen of what we were singing, they ran for the hills.

"I'm a lonely whale," I muttered, picking at a piece of chipped nail polish on my big toe.

"Speak up, girl. There's no whispering in baseball," Suze barked.

"I'm a lonely whale. No one can hear what I am really saying. Sometimes *I* can't even hear what I'm really saying."

"That's a start. There you go. Now you know it, and now you can start singing at a frequency someone can hear." Suze walked over and gave me a very aggressive hug. "I'm proud of you, champ."

Cameron flung her hand in the air.

"What do we do if we catch our boyfriend cyber cheating?" she asked.

"On the Internet? Like e-mailing?"

Cameron nodded. "But more tweeting and Facebooking."

"Ahhh, common problem these days," Suze said with a knowing nod. "All those congressmen sending out pics of their wangs and whatnot."

"But that one said he never cheated. He said it was all online. He never physically did anything."

"And would you women be cool with that?" Suze asked us, looking around the room.

Collectively we were about to shake our heads, but then we all just shrugged. We had come to accept a lot of bad behavior from dudes. If he didn't physically cheat, did it matter what he did on the Internet?

Suze groaned low and long. "Ladies, ladies, ladies. None of you have any self-respect anymore. No dignity. But I will tell you that you aren't entirely wrong. I've been doing some research for my next book: *Men: If They Didn't Have a Penis We'd Give Them Back to Their Mothers*. And oddly enough I think that we need to feel sorry for them."

This caught our attention.

"The world isn't made for men anymore. Men naturally want to be in a tribe. Think about it. They used to be the hunters and soldiers, spending nights, weeks, months, sometimes years in the company of other men. Think about men today. How often have any of your boyfriends seen their man friends? Once a week? How often do they talk on the phone except to give a few grunts and a 'Hey, meet me at the bar'?

"Never. Men no longer have camaraderie. They have no tribe."

At this Suze pounded her chest. "Women have a tribe. How often do you tell a girlfriend she is pretty or wonderful or smart in a day? How often do you e-mail or text a friend to see what she just did or to send a picture of what you just ate? All the time. Women are intimately interwoven into other women's lives. Women are validators for other women. And for men. We validate the men in our lives the same way we validate our female friends. We tell them they're handsome and strong and we listen to the mundane shit details of their boring day at the office.

"So what does this have to do with the cyber cheating? In the absence of a tribe, men go looking for outside validation elsewhere. The validation of one person isn't enough. They need more emotional support than that. We all do, but women get it from other women. Men only get a little from one woman. So they look outside their paltry tribe of two and seek emotional support from other women. When they do it online and they don't physically cheat, then they really don't see anything wrong with it. The problem is that men and women are not in the same tribe, and somehow sex, whether verbal or physical, typically happens.

"See, the world really isn't set up for these men anymore. We should feel bad for them.

"Except . . . well, except for the fact that most of them are scumbags! Am I right?" Suze jumped over Cameron's head to fist bump Prithi.

"Yes," we chorused, even though she had begun to lose us on that last rant.

"Give me a hell yes," Suze yelled. "Hell yes!" we responded with more vigor than I thought this group was capable of mustering.

With that the doorbell rang and Mikey from Crazy Eddie's walked back into the living room.

"Time for my Sunday night date, ladies." Suze winked at us, linked arms with the startled boy, and strutted out of the living room, chalk dust trailing behind her.

Become entirely ready to have a higher power remove all these defects of character

I'm not sure whose idea it was to have Dave speak at a meeting (it might have been his), but surprisingly it ended up being a really good one.

Dave was a natural-born teacher. He legitimately wanted to impart his knowledge of how men manipulate women, which was likely born of some kind of Catholic guilt about unburdening himself from all the horrible things he said and did to women. The bottle of holy water that he kept next to his bed was no longer cutting it.

He started out with a lesson on text messaging and the ways that texts are interpreted differently by men and by women.

"Men," he said, pausing for effect as he strode in front of the room like one of those prissy teachers in movies where they have to teach underprivileged kids in the ghetto, "are simple creatures. I know that you think we are very tricky and very complicated and likely playing the same mind games you are and maybe going back to our friends in the bar to dissect every text message you send us and waiting a prerequisite three days before we text you because we like you and respect you. Sometimes you think we're busy. So busy we can't take ten seconds to text you. None of that is true. No one. No one . . ." Here Dave paused for effect and pulled out his phone. He punched in a few buttons for approximately ten seconds and then held it up in the air like a trophy. "Text sent. No one is too busy to do that. If we aren't texting you, we don't like you. Period. End of story. When we like a girl, we text. We blow up her phone with texts. We're not complicated, and we don't play games.

"A lot of girls think I'm a jerk. I was an unsophisticated jerk in my early years. Sometimes I appealed to a girl's ego and I did send a ton of text messages and then maybe I would ignore her after I finally got her to juggle my balls a few times."

At this Jordana gasped. For someone so schooled in healing the human anatomy, she didn't seem to enjoy hearing about parts of it being juggled.

"But you ladies appear to be of a certain age."

Now *everyone* gasped. I was worried Dave was about to be collectively attacked by a lot of angry women he had just referred to as over the hill. I did a quick head count. Twenty ladies. This was more than he was used to taking on.

"I don't mean that as an insult. None of us are in our early twenties anymore. We have all been around the block a bit. I have become more and more honest in my older age . . . and this seems to confound your gender even more. I may have a first date with a woman and it will be great. We'll have a second date. She wonders why I don't text more or call more. We have a third date and we sleep together and she really wants to chat a lot. And I'm honest. I tell her I don't have relationships. I'm flaky. I don't really trust women. I don't see anyone longer than a fiscal quarter. Have any of you heard this before?"

There were nods . . . maybe even a few teary eyes. "Well, it's all true. We're not lying to you. But for some reason it seems to turn women on even more. Why do you like us when we are assholes? Why, I ask?" Now Dave was getting a little too into the part and punctuating all his major points with a fist or a pointer finger jabbed into the air. He was becoming Suze. I guess everyone likes an audience.

"We lay down the law. We tell it like it is. We don't think we're bad people because we are being honest. All you tell us is that you want us to be honest and share our feelings, and we do and you don't believe us.

"When do you believe us?

"When we tell you we love you after sex. You believe us when we mutter a half-guttural 'I love you' after sex. That's when we're lying to you. When we tell you we're not emotionally available and we don't want a girlfriend, that's all true. And you know what, you probably can't fix it. Maybe we do want a girlfriend and maybe we don't but if we tell you we don't want one, then we certainly don't want you to be our girlfriend. This isn't hard. It doesn't have to be hard."

At this Prithi fully burst into tears. It was either the honesty or her hormones or a combination of the two, but suddenly her giant prego body just started shaking with sobs. And Dave, the guy who had always been my friend even while he was making women cry across the tristate area, proved again that he had a heart, just not for women he was sleeping with. He walked over to Prithi and sat on the floor and just hugged her, from the front, not the side in some pussy "I don't know what to do" man hug, but a good old-fashioned bear hug, moving her head onto his shoulder and letting her cry it out. He turned around.

"Let's not let the truth hurt us anymore, ladies. Use the information I have just shared with you to take the control back in your relationships. Don't imagine yourself walking down the aisle on your first date. Do what we do. Imagine leaving in the morning after having great sex. That is my first homework assignment to you all."

Rule 6: Stop picturing your wedding day on a first date, or in Trader Joe's, or after a drunk guy at a bar sends you a text message.

"The guy you date next should just be the parsley to an already kick-ass dish of risotto. You're great the way you are. Men are just the garnish."

Jesus Christ. Dave was Dr. Phil meets Mario Batali.

And then he got a round of applause. I thanked my lucky stars I had banned him from ever sleeping with any of the women in our group. No matter how far they were coming along, every single one of them would have boned Dave that night. Despite his honesty—and he knew it.

I walked Dave out to his car. "Why do you think you treat women so badly?" Watching him in that room of women, actually seeing him enjoy interacting with women he wasn't actively trying to insert his penis into, left me confused about why he couldn't treat women he had sex with with the same respect.

Dave sighed. "I got hurt, Sophie," he said.

"I think I fell in love just once, and it hurt so bad when it ended, I decided I wouldn't let it happen again. The truth is that men aren't as strong as women. You deal with your pain by doing crazy things, but you recover. We don't bounce back the same way. When Maury dumped me right after college, I swore I would never let myself feel that bad ever again. So I go on the defensive. I say ridiculous things to women because then I know they're rejecting me because I told them they'd look hotter if they lost about ten pounds and not because of me. And I do it no matter how awesome a girl is. Every single time."

It made sense. We all had our own ways of fending off rejection.

"I listened to all those women in there," Dave continued. "Really listened to them. I don't think any of you realize what kind of power you have over us when you just drop all your insecurities. At the end of the day, you choose, and we feel lucky when you make the choice."

I gave my head a little shake. I never felt like I was the one doing the choosing or the picking.

"Don't you want to stop?" I asked him. "Maybe settle down? You're not getting any younger." I meanly flicked his growing belly.

"Maybe I should start coming to your meetings."

And that's how we got our first male member of LAA.

We were all improving. Olivia was no longer getting blackout drunk and going home with inappropriate men. Cameron had let her membership to at least twelve dating sites lapse and replaced her trolling for men by trolling for antiques and collectibles on Etsy. It was a more expensive but healthier habit and we were all gifted with recovered-wood picture frames and T-shirt scarves for being such supportive friends. The house was now a de facto halfway house for the heartbroken and lovesick, but it was turning into a lot of fun. Karaoke had become a staple, and on Saturday nights we often gathered in the basement. Sometimes Tito and Joe would join us. We learned that Tito's wife had recently left him for the local high school gym teacher, Michael Stern, who at age sixty could still do thirty-seven pull-ups in under a minute. In Mexico, where Tito's family was from, people didn't get divorced, so Tito was ashamed to admit to his family that his marriage was over and he was letting her live in the house with him (Michael had cats and she was allergic) until he got the guts to figure out another arrangement. If I didn't mention it before, Tito was gorgeous. He had mocha brown skin with the lightest crystal-blue eyes you've ever seen (the result, he told us, of a Nordic explorer great-great-grandfather who inadvertently landed on the Yucatan Peninsula).

I also learned that Joe was divorced, rather recently, but he was tight-lipped about the details, and I didn't want to push him since he wasn't officially a part of LAA, even though he was sitting in on some of the meetings and the girls often sought him out for advice as they continued to work through their personal stuff.

It was during a Saturday night sing-along that I got the call from Megan right in the middle of Princess and Tito doing a really good version of "Don't Go Breakin' My Heart" by Elton John and Kiki Dee. I answered right away, figuring Megan was planning to schedule another Suze session for us.

"Are you sitting down?" she asked. I laughed, high off Whitney Houston (although thankfully, not high *like* Whitney Houston).

"Did Suze pull the goalie with Mikey the delivery boy?"

"Huh? Oh, no, not that. I just heard something and I thought I should tell you before you found out on your own."

"Did one of your Sally Tomatoes finally get you pregnant?" This was always a concern since Megan had convinced herself that older men couldn't get her pregnant. I kept trying to explain that as unjust as it was, it didn't work the same way for men as it did for women, but she refused to listen, saying some of her paramours had a hard enough time staying, well, hard and that a condom wasn't exactly going to help things along. "OK, sure, I'm sitting down," I said, though I wasn't, the idea of bad news far away from my thoughts.

"Eric is engaged."

And all of a sudden it was back. The rubber band in my gut behind my liver. I had forgotten about it. I never even felt it anymore. The Eric cleanse was slowly but surely working. I was so focused on the group and on myself and getting caught up with work that he hadn't entered my thoughts more than a handful of times, one of which was when I found one of his ratty old gym socks static clung to the lacy black thong I had bought to impress him on his thirtieth birthday; the only thing the flimsy undies were successful in doing was giving me a rash on my backside. Now all the pain came whooshing back. I felt dizzy, and I sat down as Megan continued to tell me how she found out.

"I was having dinner in Midtown and you know I never eat up there, but I bought one of those ridiculous deals on that Groupon site for like a five-course dinner before realizing that it was in the Fifties on the East Side and you know that is no-man's-land around there. Anyway, I wasn't expecting to see anyone I knew but then he walked into the restaurant with her. His secretary. What do you call her again? Trashy McReceptionist?"

"Floozy McSecretary," I quietly replied, but not quietly enough that Annie didn't hear me from the next room and sit down next to me with alarm.

"Right, Floozy McSecretary. Anyway, obviously she bought the same Groupon. Of course she did. She seems like the kind of girl who always buys things on Groupon, doesn't she? I only bought it because it said they had two courses of cheese and you know I'm a sucker for good cheese and lots of it. So they walked in and Eric got all bashful and it looked like he was trying to push her behind a banquette or something when he saw me. He was holding her hand really tight too. He was holding it so hard I thought it looked like he was hurting her, and he was, because all of a sudden she broke out of his grip. You know she looks teensy tiny but this was like a feat of super-human strength. She broke free and began wildly gesticulating and that's when I saw it."

"The ring," I whispered.

"Yeah, the ring."

I knew the ring well. It was a two-carat princess cut from Harry Winston that had belonged to Eric's grandmother. After we had been dating for about a year, Eric's mother told me about it in confidence after she drank too much at his nephew's christening. She had just assumed that since I was dating her son at a proper age for WASPs to get married and since I was now being invited to family events (I had begged my way into that one and Eric was too hungover from a bachelor party to say no), I would likely be the recipient of said family heirloom.

"They got out of there after that," Megan continued. "Gave up the dinner and everything. Eric tried to pull me aside, I think to tell me not to tell you—he seems scared of you—but she wouldn't stop jabbering about how he hurt her hand and how she needed some ice."

The rubber band ball kept winding itself tighter.

"Sophie, are you OK? Do you want me to come out? You're not alone, are you?"

"No, I'm not alone. There's a bunch of people here, actually, so I should go. Thank you for telling me. I'm glad that I know."

I hung up the phone and laid my head down in Annie's lap, curling into a tiny ball.

"He's engaged?"

"He's engaged."

"How do you feel?"

"Bad."

"Do you want a glass of wine?"

"I think that's best."

I stayed on the floor. Annie went into the basement, probably to alert the others to my current state. After five minutes of hushed whispers, Annie returned with a glass of Chianti.

I sat up just enough to bring it to my lips and finished it with a gulp. She pulled the bottle from behind her back.

"Just finish it. Your problem is love addiction, not alcoholism. It won't kill you."

I had two more glasses before climbing to my feet.

"I'm not going to call him."

And with that, my phone rang. Speak of the devil.

"He's calling because he knows that Megan was going to tell you."

"And he's probably scared." I laughed through tears that kept threatening to spill over. "Scared that this time he really will have to take out a restraining order or something."

For the first time since Eric and I started dating, I let his call go straight to voice mail.

"I don't want to hear it from him. I don't want to hear his voice."

"'Atta girl. See how much stronger you are now? You rock. You're amazing. You're all better."

"No," I said, pouring myself another glass of wine. "If I were better, I wouldn't feel so shitty. I'm *getting* better maybe, but I'm not better."

The phone rang again, this time with seemingly greater urgency, and the tones of "I Would Do Anything for Love" blared from my handset. I had changed the ringtone from "Rump Shaker" weeks ago to remind myself of my moral inventory.

Against all better judgment I took my laptop up to my room and was only alone for fifteen minutes when Annie found me.

"Do you need a refill?"

"What do you think?"

"Well, I see you have a computer and I know how Google works . . . so do they have a wedding registry?"

"Yup."

"Fuck the Wedding Channel."

"Fuck the Wedding Channel hard."

"What are they getting?"

"A lot of things we liked . . . that I liked."

"You were the one with taste in the relationship." Annie smoothed my hair back like my mom used to do.

"I hate that these things are public," I muttered.

"I hate that you're looking at it."

"How can I not? It was one Google search away. Right there for me to find."

"Yeah, if you looked. If you put their names in with an *and*. Come on, Sophie. You're better than this right now."

I looked up at her, with wine-stained lips and a sad, sad face. "No, I am not."

She acquiesced. "No, you don't have to be." She glanced at my glass of wine with a quick hesitation followed by a determined furrow and a slight shake of her head.

"So what do these assholes want their guests to buy them?"

I proceeded to take her through the Donna Karan Lenox "Porcelain Touch" Sugar and Creamer set and the William Yeoward Country Wine Cooler . . . all the way to the Kate Spade "June Lane" two-piece dessert set.

"They're total designer whores," Annie concluded.

"They're building a life together."

"Sure, with a bunch of name-brand shit. You know what's awesome? You know what is you, Sophie? Not this crap. You may have liked this stuff when you were with him, but I can't see you in a home with this Vera Wang Wedgewood candelabra. I see you with this stuff." And she pointed downstairs. "Things that mean something. That have a history and a life and a personality. Those two are people who are trying really hard to create a personality together with a bunch of stuff. I think you liked this stuff when you were with that jerk-off who used La Mer face cream. But it was never you."

"You never said he was a jerk-off when I dated him . . ."

"Because I couldn't. Because you never would have talked to me again. Remember that time in college when I caught that other jerk-off you dated literally getting jerked off on the dance floor of your school's A-Chi-O man auction?"

"Yes."

"He high-fived me while he was getting busy with her, but you didn't return my calls for a month until you finally caught him in bed with two Alpha Chi Omega sisters, one of whom had a very unfortunate mustache."

"I was young and stupid," I said very quietly.

"And now I realize that you aren't anymore. And I can say things that will make you angry and in the morning you can't get away from me anymore. You have to sit and look at me over the breakfast table and accept what I said. Eric sucked some giant balls. You pandered to him in every way. But you are getting over him. And in the past few weeks, I have seen you be stronger and happier than I have seen you in years, so I need you to stop staring at this list of sad department store consumerist bullshit and feeling sorry for yourself. They may have a life filled with $65 towels, but he will still suck, and I guarantee you that you will not be the last girl he cheated on."

I nodded slowly.

"If you want, we can buy everything on this registry and then return it so that they end up getting nothing," Annie said in all seriousness.

"Nope. That's not the kind of girl I am anymore. Or at least, that's not the kind of girl I *want* to be anymore," I said, and I meant it. "But that is a really excellent revenge-filled idea and someday I hope you get to suggest it to someone who has gone through less personal growth."

Annie kissed me on the forehead and walked out of the room, confident that she would see me at the breakfast table in the morning.

I thought I had drifted off to sleep, but then I heard Joe's voice. "Hey, Sophie, do you want to talk about it?"

I shook my head.

"Do you want us to leave?"

I shook my head again. I still had the remnants of the wine. I wanted to suckle at the bottle while I lay down. About a half hour later, Joe knocked on the door again with a glass of water.

"We don't have to talk about you," he said.

"OK," I slurred slightly.

He perched at the end of the bed and gently exchanged my wine bottle for his water glass. "I never told you the story about my divorce?" he said with the hint of a question mark at the end.

"Nope, you never did."

"Well, now's as good a time as any," he said with a light laugh. "One thing that never changes is misery loving company. The best way to feel better about a shit situation is to hear about someone else's shit situation."

"I want to hear about it," I murmured, because he was right. The only thing I wanted to hear about at this moment was how someone else had become unhappy.

"My parents met in college at Indiana State. He played football and she was on the dance squad. They got married three weeks after graduation and have been married for the past forty years. I have never seen two people more in love with each other. I mean, I walked in on them having sex."

"Gross! But everyone walks in on their parents having sex when they're kids. It's one of those grail tests of horror we're forced to endure in order to build character or something."

"I walked in on them having sex last weekend."

"Oh, God, old sex. That's really gross!"

"But kind of great, right? The fact that my parents in their sixties are still having all sorts of sex."

I reconsidered. It was kind of great, in a gross way.

"Anyway, my entire life I wanted what they had. I wanted their fairy tale marriage with that amount of closeness and so that was what I was looking for when I went away to college. And when I started dating Elizabeth, I figured it had to be her because she was my college girlfriend and she was great on paper and she seemed to want all the same things I wanted. I thought, *Great, now I get to check this off my list.* This was easy and now I'll live happily ever after like my parents. We moved to New York after school so Liz could go to law school. I decided to go to med school at NYU instead of Yale because Columbia was the best school she got in to. We lived on the

Upper West Side to be close to her campus. We decided to get married after we both graduated from school. While we were studying we barely saw each other, so when we did, everything was perfectly fine. Once we got married and we had a little more time to be a couple, something didn't feel right. In fact, I barely knew this girl. I barely knew myself. I hadn't been alone since I was eighteen years old and now I was stuck living this life with a stranger. We were nothing like my mom and dad. We never had sex. Neither of us ever seemed to want to. I always imagined coming home and cracking open a bottle of wine with my young wife and trading stories about our day while we cooked dinner and laughed before falling into each other's arms and making love all night long. But most of the time Liz would go out with her girlfriends from law school, and I would crack open a bottle of whiskey and pass out on the couch."

"Is that when you started drinking a lot?"

"I was drinking more often than I wasn't drinking. What put me over the edge was when she cheated on me."

I put my hand to my mouth. "Did you catch her?"

"I accidentally answered her phone one afternoon when she was in the shower. It was him."

"How did people ever catch cheaters before cell phones?"

That at least made him laugh a little.

"But the drinking got worse after the separation because I felt like such a failure."

I looked up at Joe who was perched on the edge of my bed and he looked so sad. The crinkles around his eyes got more pronounced and his mouth twisted into a funny shape with his lower lip curving over his left incisor.

"My divorce was only officially final last week. I didn't sign the papers right away. Her lawyer kept calling me and her parents called me, but for the first six months I was too drunk to sign anything, then I was too angry, and then I just gave up."

I sat up so I could look him in the eyes. I finally felt bad about lying there while he was telling me the saddest bedtime story of all time.

"But she was a bad fish," I said.

"She was my only fish. It was the only time I ever dove," Joe said, seeming to brighten because I remembered his fish tale. "I think that next time I'll be a lot more careful."

"Do you think you'll have the courage to dive again?"

"I do. When the time is right."

And then, without thinking about it, I leaned in and I kissed him. At first he stiffened, before loosening his lips and letting me slide my tongue into his mouth and my arms around his neck, and then for a minute he was kissing me back—hungrily, it felt like, before he pulled away.

"We shouldn't. You just found out your cheating ex is getting married and I . . . I have so much to work on myself."

"You've been more than six months sober," I pointed out, eager to keep going. But Joe was firm. "Sophie, you're a little bit drunk."

Oh my God. I had just kissed a recovering alcoholic, my breath positively reeking of cheap Chianti. He probably dove into my mouth remembering all sorts of boozy memories. I was a horrible person. He couldn't have possibly wanted to kiss me.

"I want to kiss you," he said, as if he were reading my mind. "Now just isn't the best time for either of us to dive in, and you know that." I did know it. But I was buoyed by the fact that he said that he wanted to kiss me. For now, that was enough for me.

"Get some sleep, Sophie. I promise all this is going to feel a lot easier in the morning."

I shuffled my way under the blankets still in my clothes and polished off the glass of water Joe had brought into my room. He kissed me lightly on the forehead.

"Sweet dreams," he whispered and padded out the door.

What seemed like minutes later but had to have been at least six hours, I heard a wail. "Get up. Get up all of you!" It jolted me out of my uncharacteristically sound (and drunken) sleep.

It was dark, and all I could hear was Jordana screeching. When she flicked on my overhead light, I could see she had a cowbell in one hand, a bottle of champagne in the other, and she was wearing the most spectacular party dress I had ever seen somewhere other than a red carpet event on television. She looked like Jessica Rabbit with all the sequins and bosoms I didn't realize she had. Even though she had an obvious addiction to sugar, I didn't take her for a very heavy drinker. Through my crusty sleep-filled eyes, I could see the bottle wasn't even open.

"You must all get your arses out of bed and put on your finest clothes. It's an order." When someone British says something like that, it does sound like a direct order from the Queen or

Dumbledore in *Harry Potter* and you end up moving involuntarily to do whatever it is the person barked.

"You can't wear that," she said to me about the jeans and T-shirt I was still wearing from the night before. "It isn't appropriate. Put on your nicest party dress and meet me downstairs in ten. What we are about to do is going to change your life."

Jordana had apparently given her spiel to everyone in the house because within ten minutes, the family room looked like a group getting ready to go to a cougar prom.

"No shoes. Everyone take off the shoes. I don't know what you were thinking," Jordana instructed.

When a bat shit Brit asks you to put on your finest outfit at midnight, you should never include a pair of Jimmy Choos. I don't know what any of us *had* been thinking. How was it possible that she was making us feel like we were the ones completely out of our minds?

"OK, you will all follow me in a single file line. I promise we are going to return to this house changed women."

And so we marched in a single file line out of the house and down the street and down four more streets and finally up onto the boardwalk.

"Jordana, we can't go on the beach now. It's not allowed until sunrise."

"Lucky for us we are only about ten minutes from sunrise and I don't think anyone will begrudge us ten little minutes, certainly not this town's Keystone Kops."

We walked onto the beach, pleased we had ditched the heels

for flip-flops, but we were a little chilly in the ocean breeze in the party dresses and all, especially Prithi, who really wasn't wearing much of anything at all. Her party dress was obviously from her prematernity days so what was once a knee-length tube dress barely covered her midsection and enormous boobs.

Jordana instructed us all to line up. I thought, *If she tells us to go into downward dog right now, I might actually throw her into the ocean.*

"Ladies, we are approaching a very important moment in our lives. For the past couple of months each and every one of you has given me strength, a strength I didn't know I had or that I would ever need. I know that every single one of you has come a long way on your journeys. Well, now, right now actually, is a pivotal moment in all our journeys. I have brought you here on the cusp of the autumnal equinox, the start of fall, one of two days of the year when we have exactly as much day as we have night. Starting in five minutes, we will have exactly twelve hours of sunlight followed by exactly twelve hours of night. The day is in perfect balance. It is our duty to embrace this divine moment. From here on we will be thankful for our blessings and abundance and make the decision to continue to grow as new women."

Jordana popped the cork and instructed Stella, who was first in our ragtag line, to tip her head backward. She poured just a drop of champagne into each of our mouths, except for Annie's, and her words actually inspired us to shriek like banshees in celebration. It was as if we had all been taken over by the spirits

142

of the equinox. We yelled at the sea, sticky from champagne and gritty with sand, party dresses dragging in the foam as we watched the sun emerge to begin its twelve-hour journey across the earth to start out its perfectly balanced day.

Jordana came up behind me and put her long limbs around me in a bear hug. "You get to be a new you starting today. It's a gift."

She was right. I just had to figure out how to use it.

Humbly ask our higher power to remove our shortcomings (fix us, please!)

One day Stella simply started talking again, and once she started there was no shutting her up. Her voice was a surprise. For such a reedy girl, it was low and throaty. But more than that, she was funny. Her jokes were more often than not dirty, and she liked to shock by making references to bizarre sexual acts that most of the time we had never heard of.

Don't even get me started on how she used "donkey punch."

In the week since Megan had informed me of Eric's impending nuptials, I had contemplated calling him exactly thirteen and a half times. (The half was the time I contemplated calling Floozy.)

I knew how many times I almost called because I had documented it on the blackboard in the basement for everyone to see, my own kind of scarlet (chalk) moral inventory of shame.

It was a good reminder to myself of what I was up against. I had been an idiot to think that years and years of love and boyfriend addiction and bad breakups could be erased in three months.

My shame was next to another blackboard where we had begun to catalog our deal breakers in relationships to remind ourselves that we deserved better than the losers we had dated in the past.

Men who play video games

Men who wear socks with sandals

Men who use LOL in texts

Men who will have sex with you but refuse to kiss you

Men with small dogs

Men who text their mom "nighty, nighty, moo, moo" every
    night before bed

Men who ask you if you're taking "baby killing medicine" after
    you have sex

Men who want to be tickled

Men who ask you to pee on them

Men who call you a retarded slut

I hadn't heard from Joe since the night of the sloppy kiss. I knew he was still coming over to chat with Annie, but he hadn't made any special trips around the house to see me.

I was an enormous idiot, first, for thinking that he was into me and, second, for throwing myself at a recovering alcoholic while I was drunk. Joe wasn't looking for a hot mess. Joe was looking for the love of his life, a big juicy fish that was worth taking a dive for, and I was just a clammy sea urchin knocking back one too many seaweed-tinis.

While I was falling off the wagon, Annie was steadily perched atop hers. She hadn't had a drink in ninety days, had attended copious "meetings" and one-on-one counseling sessions, and was about to go before the judge to find out if she could get her license back. Dave and I sprawled on her bed as she primped to learn her fate.

"Will you drive me to court, Sophie?" she asked, properly attired in a striking pink pencil skirt and white blouse that I figured she borrowed from Princess specially for the occasion.

"Will Joe be there?"

"Why? Are you going to tongue rape him again?"

"Uncool, Annie," Dave said. "Dude rape is a thing."

"I knew I shouldn't have told you what happened!" I moaned.

Dave continued as if I weren't wailing with emotional angst. "One time I drank a lot of absinthe at a party in the aquarium. I thought I was making out with a mermaid and I woke up in the morning in bed with a sea lion. I think she dude raped me."

It was Annie's turn to ignore Dave. "You did it in a moment of weakness," she said to me in reference to the kiss, or maybe in reference to telling her about it.

I didn't want to ask, but I couldn't help myself. "Has he mentioned me when you talk to him?"

"Nope. But we don't talk about him. We talk about me. That's what counseling is all about, and yes, he will be there. He

is testifying on my behalf. Come on. You know that he probably thinks this whole thing is very funny. He's the kind of guy
who forgives stupid mistakes. And you're gonna have to see
him one of these days."

"OK, I'll drive you. But I need something better to wear.
Where's Princess?"

An hour and four dresses later, I walked into the judge's
chambers with Dave and Annie wearing a printed wrap dress
that would have shown off décolletage if I'd had any to show.
It wasn't at all like a trial, more like a group of people sitting
around a living room preparing to give an errant child a lecture.
The pretty female bailiff cast Dave a withering glance.

"What'd you do to that one?" I hissed.

"I made the mistake of telling her I only dated girls that were
either really hot or remarkably brilliant."

"That sounds flattering."

"She asked which one she was."

"What the hell did you say?"

"I said she certainly wasn't a rocket scientist . . . turkey."

I still didn't know what Dave meant when he called his poor
victims turkeys, but whatever it did mean, I was sure it wasn't
flattering.

Old Judge Turner first asked Annie about her family and,
strangely enough, her bar, and after twenty-five minutes moved
on to her probation.

"Annie, do you think that you have fulfilled all the obliga-
tions of your probation?"

"I do, Judge Turner," Annie said with a smile so sickeningly sweet I wanted to laugh, but I could tell the judge was just eating it up.

"Do you think you're still a menace to this good town of ours? Have you learned your lesson about drinking too much?"

"I'm not and I have, with the help of my wonderful counselor."

Judge Turner turned to Joe, who had been sitting in the chambers when I arrived and hadn't so far even glanced back at me.

"Doctor, would you mind answering a few questions?"

"Of course not, Your Honor."

"What have you seen these past ninety days in your counseling sessions with Annie?"

"I've seen a woman who was very dedicated to her recovery . . . once she finally admitted she had a problem. Admitting that took a while for her, but it takes a while for anyone. Once she knew what her demons were, she was ready to tackle them head-on."

"And have you seen any signs of relapse, Doctor?"

At this, Joe finally turned and half looked at me.

"All of us get close to relapsing, and all of us continue to grapple with bad judgment. But Annie has consistently made the right decisions, even when she has been put in situations that would have caused her to lapse back into bad behavior."

Now Joe looked me square in the eyes and gave a half smile, one that was almost sheepish and made the grooves around his eyes move in miniature smiles along his temples.

"Would you recommend that her probation be lifted?"

"I would recommend that she continue in her rehabilitation

program because I think that it has helped her enormously and I think she gains strength from it, but yes, I think she is ready for her probation to be lifted."

I was holding my breath waiting to find out if Annie was going to get her life back, but I also needed to know whether my probation was going to be lifted.

Could Joe and I go back to just being friends and forget the fact that I drunkenly kissed him after finding out my ex-boyfriend was marrying his secretary?

"Well, Annie, I hereby lift your probation. Please don't go stealing any cop cars, and stay away from Mrs. Dinkdorf's cat."

"Woot!" Annie whooped as she practically dove over the wide mahogany desk to hug Judge Turner, her pencil skirt creeping up to reveal a bright purple thong. I blushed on her behalf as I walked next to Joe and held out my hand in congratulations.

"Nice job, Doctor."

He reached out to shake the proffered palm before enveloping me in a bear hug.

"I'm sorry," he whispered in my ear, his breath cool on the lobe.

"What for?" I asked.

"Let's talk later," he said, nodding at Annie who had turned to tackle Joe.

"I can drive my motherfucking car! Sorry, Your Honor, but I can DRIVE. MY. MOTHER. FUCKING. CAR!"

Joe agreed to leave his car at the courthouse in order to let Annie drive the two of us home.

"Does this mean you want to get a drink, An?" I asked.

"Not even a little, to tell you the truth. I feel pretty great being sober. You know, I never really got hangovers . . ."

Joe and I nodded. This was a point of pride for Annie.

"But I never felt a hundred percent, either. You know, Frank Sinatra used to say that he felt bad for sober people because that was the best they were going to feel all day. I used to drink to feel better, but now, three months off the sauce, I always feel pretty good."

"I feel pretty good too," I declared without being asked. "Look, I'll just admit it to you both. I wasn't great when I heard the news about Eric and Lacey. Yes, her name is Lacey. I am now using her real name. And I wanted to call him and that was wrong." I turned. "And, Joe, I put my tongue in your mouth." At that, Joe laughed.

"Sophie," he said through a giggle. "That wasn't a capital offense. So you kissed me. You were drunk."

"But you're a recovering alcoholic. That makes me a jerk."

"Do you think I kissed you back because your lips tasted like wine?"

Wait, he kissed me back? He had said it before, but saying it again meant it was likely true. I didn't know what to say. But at that, Annie changed the subject the way she tends to do when attention is deflected away from her.

"Let's have a party tonight to celebrate. I'll get some of the cooks from the bar to come over and make us dinner. We'll fire up the karaoke machine and call some of the girls in from the city. It will be a very sober celebration of being sober. Except you guys can drink if you really want to. Oooo, I want to get a dartboard for the house. Do you think we could get a dartboard? I don't know why, but I just got an incredible urge to play some darts."

I happened to know that Alan and Chris, Annie's arresting officers, had gotten her a deluxe dartboard as a ninety-days-sober present and that they were planning to bring it by tonight, after they made sure all went well with the judge.

"Ha. Let's get some food first and then we can look into a dartboard."

Everyone was on board with the party, and soon it felt like half the town had come out to celebrate Annie being off probation, being allowed to go back and work in her bar if she so chose, and the fact that she was ready to start a new life. Three of Annie's ex-girlfriends even showed up, all of them following her around like lovesick puppies. I was tempted to tell them about LAA before deciding it would be a conflict of interest. Tito had managed to make a screen using a large white sheet rigged to the back fence so that the lyrics for karaoke were projected large enough for everyone to see across the yard to sing along. While he was hauling it downstairs from the linen closet I saw him pause on the stairs to give Katrina a whack on the backside. She didn't protest. I didn't know what that was all about. Tito certainly wasn't her type. He was *all* man.

There was singing and dancing until midnight, when the neighbors with small kids politely asked us to keep things down. And through the entire evening Annie didn't take a single drink.

She did learn that she sucked at darts sober, but I think Chris and Alan let her win a couple of times so she wouldn't feel so bad.

Joe was a social butterfly all night, and every time I thought we might get a chance to be alone, one of us was interrupted by someone else bubbling up about how nice a time they were having or trying to pull one of us onto the makeshift stage to sing with them. Before I knew it, I was heading upstairs to fall asleep, leaving the cleaning until the morning and any resolution with Joe, well, unresolved.

Make a list of all the persons (exes) we have harmed, and become willing to make amends

Making amends is a big part of any twelve-step program. Because addicts (even love addicts) tend to leave behind them a trail of emotional wreckage, it is important to identify the people who have been hurt along the way and try to do justice to that relationship that was breached. Amends are like a step up from an apology. You have to really mean it and try to make it right.

It's a nice thing to do for other people, but it's also about your own emotional healing. Admitting you have wronged someone helps take away some of the shame you have been feeling.

This started a long discussion about whom we should make amends to.

How did we determine if we had actually hurt someone?

I had been pondering amends on a Thursday night as I walked the five blocks from my grandmother's to Matt and

Robert's. My high school boyfriend and his husband had heard about LAA through the town gossip mill and wanted a complete download. Robert is something of a gourmet chef so there was no way I was going to say no to dinner in their completely fabulous renovated Craftsman.

It was chilly for the first week in October and I wished I had worn a sweater over the halter top I was certain Matt would be judgy about. I gave myself a little mental pat on the back that I was wearing a truly excellent pair of Tory Burch flats procured from Princess's extensive collection. As I glanced down to admire them I noticed an inscription on the sidewalk that had been there about as long as I could remember.

Someone had scratched "Ally loves Pete" in the sidewalk cement on Eleanor's corner about ten years ago. I didn't know Ally or Pete but I always speculated about their semi-permanent declaration of love and where they were now. Did they meet in high school like Matt and me and make it through college, relationship intact, save for a three-month break when Ally flirted with the idea of making out with girls and Pete had a night of debauchery with his English professor? Did they come back to town after college, get married, and start a family here? I played the "Ally and Pete: Where are they now?" game all the way to Matt's.

"Hey, S. B. Hawk!" Matt greeted me, smiling as he used his tenth-grade nickname for me, based on the singer Sophie B. Hawkins. Her one hit, "Damn, I Wish I Was Your Lover," was playing the first time we had awkward sex in the bedroom of my parents' house while they were at some kind of conference for my dad's job in Arizona. Ironic, I know.

"Hey, D. Mc." I countered with a familiar moniker. DMc stood for Dylan McKay. As I mentioned before, Matt had a thing for *90210*.

Matt and Robert are one of those painfully perfect couples. They both stand just over six feet and have the same wiry but muscled builds, which allowed them to double their wardrobes of John Varvatos and Marc Jacobs when they moved in together. The gays just have everything figured out.

Michael Buble was playing on what I knew were hidden wireless speakers and Robert was tasting from a bowl of ceviche I was sure he had lovingly begun marinating in lime hours earlier.

"Hon"—he motioned for Matt to come over—"do you think this needs more cilantro?"

Matt strode over and took a mouthful from Robert's proffered spoon.

"Oh, my God." My ex-boyfriend moaned in a way that was oddly familiar and vaguely uncomfortable. "No, baby. It is perfect. Just perfect." He turned around and gave his husband a kiss on the mouth.

"Now I want some!" I smiled. Robert proceeded to spoon-feed me, too. I could never tell how much Robert really liked me. I wasn't sure if he humored me because I was part of Matt's history or if he was grateful to me because I was probably the woman who helped my ex finally come out of the closet.

My "help" in this area came up once we were eating our first course of risotto on the boys' back deck.

"Did I ever do anything to hurt you while we were dating?" I asked Matt.

"You mean besides losing tape 11?" Matt said, raising one of his elegantly shaped eyebrows. "Because that was painful for me."

"I will be sorry about tape 11 until I am an old lady in a nursing home somewhere, but no, that's not what I mean. Like, did I ever do something really bad to you?"

"You forced me out of the closet. That wasn't great," Matt said.

"What do you mean I forced you? You came out when we broke up."

Robert, sensing that there was about to be drama, started clearing away the plates.

"Darling," Matt began in an even tone, "I am not mad at you. I want to say that from the beginning. But you were a wicked little bitch when I broke up with you. You told the entire school that you thought I was gay because you felt shitty about our breakup."

My hand went to my mouth. "I didn't tell the whole school you were gay." But then I remembered how things went down thirteen years earlier. Matt, always the gentleman, had come to my parents' house and taken me for a walk down to the beach. He held my hand and told me that he didn't think we were right for each other. I naturally began sobbing. I was losing the love of my life, the man that I was definitely going to marry and have babies with. My romantic future had ended before it even had a chance to really begin.

After Matt walked me home, I called Annie, who was in Florida for the weekend with her dad and her uncles, to commiserate.

"He's gay," Annie said. "I think Matt is just gay for breaking up with you. He doesn't like chicks."

Now remember that this was 1999. Ellen had come out to Oprah only two years earlier. *Glee* hadn't happened yet. Ricky from *My So-Called Life* was still considered a borderline pariah. High school lacrosse players in the New Jersey suburbs just didn't come out of the closet until college. Gay, and I hate myself now for saying this, was still an insult. Those were dark times.

And so that seed was planted in my head. I was angry and I was vindictive. I hated that Matt had rejected me. Whenever one of my girlfriends would talk to me about the breakup (which was near constant because I couldn't shut up about it), I would end the conversation by shrugging my shoulders and laughing as I said, "Maybe he's gay."

The problem was Matt *was* gay and he thought that I knew. (I didn't.) So within the month, he told his parents and eventually our friends at school. Matt Siggman was one of the most confident men that I knew. Once he made the decision to no longer hide who he was, he legitimately changed the way people thought of gay people in our town. He was still captain of the lacrosse team, but he was out and he was proud. Two more guys from the team came out the following year, and shortly after, our high school was one of the first in the country to start an LGBT alliance—all good things to come out of me being a crazy little bitch, right?

I must have spaced as I remembered how things went down because Matt was pinching a little bit of chub at my hip.

"S. B. Hawk, hey, you! That was a long time ago. I have forgiven you. You were a 'see you next Tuesday' but maybe that is how things were supposed to go. My life is infinitely better for having come out of the closet in high school," Matt said. "I went into college as a poised and confident gay man. Maybe I should thank you."

I looked up at my adorable high school boyfriend. "No. I need to apologize. I have never apologized to you for the things I said and did after our breakup but now I will. I am sorry, and I mean that from the bottom of my heart."

I did mean it. There was no excuse, besides being seventeen, to have behaved so badly and lashed out in such a vehement way just because a relationship was coming to its natural end. I thought of the next rule for our LAA group.

Rule 7: Sometimes things just end, and that has to be OK. You don't always (sometimes it is justified) have to be a "see you next Tuesday" about it.

We hugged it out. Robert reemerged from the kitchen with an entire raspberry truffle cheesecake in a pie tin.

"For the rest of the lovelorn," he said, presenting it to me.

"Cheesecake, Robert? You've watched too many episodes of *The Golden Girls*," I teased, eagerly accepting the cake.

Robert nodded. "It's true. In high school, I managed to tape all the reruns of *Golden Girls* off Nick at Nite."

I was genuinely happy that my first love had found his perfect soul mate.

I was still a little foggy from Robert's impeccably curated wine pairings when there was a knock on my bedroom door, around 2:30 a.m. This time it was unaccompanied by a cowbell.

I sat up with a start. Princess and Nahla rolled over simultaneously, their matching pink sleep masks inching up their noses as they shifted their weight to their right sides. My first thought was that it was Joe. That he finally wanted to be alone with me and talk about things. I adjusted my white tank top so that it showed a bit more cleavage (why was I constantly kidding myself?) and yelled, "Come in."

"Stella is missing." This was the second time Jordana had come to my room in the dead of night, but now she was more concerned than crazy.

"What do you mean missing?" I asked.

"I mean missing. She didn't come to bed, and I thought maybe she was staying up writing in her journal. I even thought, Ooohhh, maybe she has a dalliance going with Dr. Twelve Steps." Dr. Twelve Steps was obviously Joe and that one hurt like a sharp jab in my side.

"But after midnight I got nervous so I riffled through her things and found her wallet missing, and a duffel."

Princess sleeps like a log due to an intense herbal regimen

she swallows before bed, so it took three tries to shake her awake as well as a sleepy growl from Nahla, who was also displeased at having her beauty rest disrupted.

"Stella's missing. We think she left."

Realizing there was a problem that she could potentially help solve, possibly with her intuitive powers, crystals, and some chanting, Princess came to pretty easily, ordered us to put a pot of coffee on the stove, and said she would meet us downstairs in fifteen minutes after she "got herself together." I never imagined there was a proper outfit for being woken up in the middle of the night to search for a missing house-mate, but I now know it involves mules and a coordinated twin set.

Jordana rallied the other house members, and fifteen minutes later we were all sitting in the living room when we heard Princess shriek and went running to our room. Maybe there was a crazed killer in the house. Maybe he had staged it to look like Stella ran away but he had really dragged her off in the dead of night and now he was after Princess.

Princess was staring at the makeshift closet she had constructed for the overflow of her things.

"Christian is missing. My Christian Louboutin heels are missing," she said with a low rumble in her tone that indicated she would stab a bitch for stealing her shoes. She would have given them to anyone who asked, probably even a stranger on the street, but the impropriety of taking without asking was simply too much for Princess to bear.

"So we have a kidnapper and a thief on our hands," Jordana said, sighing. "I'm calling the police."

And then a feeling of clarity washed over me. "How long has Stella been here?" I asked.

"About ten weeks," Annie said.

"And what day is today?"

"It's Sunday. Very, very early Sunday morning."

My hand clasped to my mouth in my "Aha!" moment. "She's going to the tulip ceremony. She's going to stop the Husband from proposing to someone else on live national television. It's the only thing that makes sense. She snuck out in the dead of night. She took Katrina's hottest shoes. She must have gotten ahold of an Internet connection at some point and found out the latest on the show and snapped. But the question is where's the ceremony?"

Joe, who had crashed on the couch downstairs after the party, now emerged from the basement, looking adorable in the bottoms of scrubs and a worn NYU T-shirt that must have been at least ten years old and was probably as soft as kitten fur.

"New York." We all turned toward him, surprised he was the one supplying us with this information. "The final tulip ceremony is taking place in New York this year, on top of the Empire State Building, in some homage to *Sleepless in Seattle* and *An Affair to Remember*. The producers have been building it up all season. I guess the ratings have been slipping since none of the Husbands ever turn into a real husband—they all end up on *Dancing with Celebrities* or *Famous People Rehab*—so they decided to make this tulip ceremony more dramatic. Both women have a time to be on the roof. The Husband comes up to the roof for the one he's chosen. The other just gets left up there all alone like the strange alternative plot of a poorly written romantic comedy." Joe began to look a little sheepish for knowing so many details about the show's final episode when he saw all of our heads cocked to the side in wonder.

He tried to explain. "When Stella came and talked to me about her situation, as her counselor I felt like I should be familiar with what she was battling against, so I started watching at my place." Then he admitted, "Once I started I couldn't stop. The show is addictive. He just keeps dumping these women on national television and the ones remaining just keep getting nastier and nastier each episode until finally there are only the two nastiest, most cunning ones left, but he doesn't know it because he only spends like an hour with each of them at a time."

I cut him off. "You don't have to explain. We all know how addictive reality dating shows can be. Now we know where she went. We just need to figure out how to stop her before she completely embarrasses herself or gets arrested for whatever it is she's planning."

"Who's coming with me? We can fit three more in my car."

All ten hands went into the air.

Jordana spoke up. "I think we're all coming. We're all in this together."

Joe, looking for a way to redeem his momentarily lost manhood, piped up. "I have the keys to the hospital's geriatrics van. I think that will fit all of us."

We drove to Manhattan in silence, with Jordana curled around the wheelchair lift on the floor. We went directly to my old apartment, which I hadn't visited in more than three months. I figured we could use it as a base of operations.

I don't know why, but I had had the foresight to straighten up before abandoning the place, so fortunately there were no granny panties lying around. I did feel like I was entering the apartment of a girl I didn't know very well. Could I really have changed so much in three months? Pictures of Eric and me still covered every available surface. Why did I ever want to look at him that much? Or at anyone that much for that matter. I felt a little twinge of guilt when I saw Joe look at what had to be the tenth photo of Eric and me posing in front of something silly: the Empire State Building, the Statue of Liberty, a naked guy playing the guitar in Times Square. It was as if I had to keep taking pictures of the two of us in front of things that were real to prove we were real. If I could just see it in glossy print, then everything must be OK. The thing is that a picture does tell a thousand words, a thousand words we are too scared to tell ourselves about why we insisted on taking it in the first place. These pictures were all forced fun, and you could see it on Eric's face. I remembered the one in Times Square. It was freezing, which was too bad for that naked cowboy, and Eric was begging me to just get in a cab with him, but I insisted and finally found a

Japanese tourist who spoke English and agreed to take the picture. In it I am smiling maniacally, so pleased to be getting proof of our day together. Eric is looking off into the distance. At the time, when I first printed the photo out, I told myself he was being reflective about our wonderful time. Now I could see he was looking for a way to escape the moment.

It was almost four a.m. by the time we got settled and started to form some kind of game plan for the following morning. My fridge miraculously still held several not bad blocks of cheese in addition to all the contents that should have been disposed of weeks earlier, so I was able to create the semblance of a cheese plate for us to snack on while we decided what to do. One of Jordana's private clients was a producer with ABC, the network that aired *The Husband*, and Jordana knew that she typically got up around six a.m. to do a lap around the reservoir with her Wheaton terrier, Bosco. She didn't want to call or text her, worried that would set off alarm bells, so she planned to stage a run-in in the park to try to pump her for information about what time the producers would begin setting up for the grand finale.

Before we left, Princess mentioned that Tito once told her his brother worked security at the Empire State Building. She sent him a text and then explained to us that they exchanged numbers once when she told him she was worried about Nahla eating one of the plants in the garden that had what she thought were poisonous berries.

Now we just had to wait for Jordana's client and Tito to wake up so we could figure out our next steps. Everyone seemed content to find a spot and a pillow and curl up in my small living room so I migrated to my old bedroom. I ran my hand over the teddy bear that Eric had won me at Coney Island, one of the only presents he had ever given me and the result of a bearded lady egging him on by saying he threw like a girl. He spent $50 to win that scrappy bear, just to save his ego. Why didn't any of these things bother me when we were together? Love goggles were the only answer. Like having seven beers, everything looks prettier and fuzzier about a person when we think we are in love with him or her.

I heard a soft knock and thought that I really should offer the other half of the bed to someone else since we had so much work to do tomorrow morning. When I cracked the door, I saw it was Joe.

"Can I come in?" he asked shyly.

"Of course. Welcome to my world, my other world. It feels like a whole other life."

"You've come really far in the past three months. You've learned a lot about yourself. That's a hard thing to do. Trust me, I've been trying to do it too."

"I'm sorry about all the Eric pictures," I said, not knowing entirely why I was apologizing to Joe. What did he care that my apartment was filled with gigantically cheesy photos of me and my ex-boyfriend?

"No need to apologize for anything. The girl in those pictures looks like she's trying really hard to be happy." At first I was amazed that he knew me so well, but then I remembered that, as a shrink, it was his job to know.

"She thought she was happy."

"But she wasn't?"

"Not really, no. It's like she—it's like I—had a fantasy about what things should be like and was working really hard to make it all come true. And when it didn't, I was faking it to try to make it."

Joe lay down on the bed above the covers. He patted the space next to him in such a chaste way I would have been disappointed if I hadn't been so exhausted. But as I lay down he curled his arm under my waist and pulled my head into the little nook between his shoulder and his breastbone. I had always tried to snuggle my head into this exact space on Eric's chest, but it never fit. I was always being poked by an errant bone sticking out somewhere that didn't correspond with the shape of my head. But stubborn me kept trying. I couldn't even count how many sleepless nights I spent trying to fit my head into that space where nature didn't want it to go and how many little bruises I had around my temples from trying to force it to fit.

"If you had a boat, what would you name it?" Joe asked me. This man loved non-sequitur storytelling.

"I don't know. I've never thought about getting a boat," I replied, playing along because I liked the space my head was nestled into.

"Me neither. I get horrible seasickness."

"Then why would you name a boat?"

"That's the thing. The only reason I want a boat is to give it a name. It's really the only thing besides your kid that you get to name, and unlike with kids, you can give it a crazy name. Like Apple Pie Lovey."

"You can name your kids that if you're a celebrity."

"True, but I'm not a celebrity. I'm a poor drunk doctor in New Jersey."

"OK, so what would you name your boat?"

Joe was obviously excited to talk about his imaginary boat and he began to ramble. As he talked I realized how much I adored these tangents he would go off on. They were soothing, and they demonstrated that he actually gave a lot of thought to things.

"One time I was in this little Sicilian fishing village on a tiny island off the western coast of the island called Marettimo, and all the boats there had names about the moon: *Piccolo Luna—Little Moon, Grande Luna—Big Moon, Blanca Luna—White Moon*. Beautiful, right?"

"Yeah."

"And then in the middle of all the moons, the *Puttana Grossa*."

"The what?"

"The *Fat Whore*. It belonged to a fisherman named Pippo, who got the boat after his wife ran away with his business partner, Marco. They went to the next island to raise goats. So every time Pippo would circle that other island, passing the goat farm, he would honk the horn, pull down his pants, literally moon his ex-wife, and then point to the name of the boat."

This made me laugh so hard I had to catch myself when I remembered there were people sleeping in the other room who had to get up in a couple of hours.

"So are you telling me you would name your boat something crazy after your ex-wife? *Elizabeth Is a Slut* or some such?"

"No. I'm not angry at her anymore. Plus, why would I give her the satisfaction of naming my boat after her?"

I switched gears for a minute. "What's Marettimo like?"

"It's the most beautiful place in the world. Picture these untouched white cliffs plunging into water that alternates between turquoise and emerald green."

"It sounds like paradise. But Pippo still wanted revenge. He couldn't be happy in the most beautiful place in the world?"

"Love makes people crazy, Sophie. You know that better than anyone. I think the *Puttana Grossa* was his version of, say, putting a naked picture of his wife on the Internet."

I gasped and turned red, before realizing he didn't actually know that I had done something like that. He must have just been using it as an example. I hoped he was just using it as an example.

"You'd love Marettimo," he murmured. "I'd love to see it again sober. We should go there sometime."

The use of that pronoun—*we*—gave me flutters in my belly of the happy sort I hadn't felt in years. But the flutters were quickly followed by a twinge of warning: DO NOT GET AHEAD OF YOURSELF, SOPHIE.

I thought for a minute.

"I would name mine *Serenity Luna*."

"*Serenity Moon*? That's nice," Joe said, burying his face in my hair.

As I listened to his breathing get shallower, I decided not to admit to him that I thought the *Floozy McSecretary* sounded like a jaunty name. Of course, Eric didn't have a goat farm and I couldn't exactly ride my boat around his office building. The closest I could come would be to rent an ad on the side of a taxicab. But that would be ridiculous. And anyway, the thought didn't give me the same satisfaction my former revenge plots had in the past. I pushed it out of my head to fall asleep thinking about towering cliffs, green and blue water, and the word *we*.

I thought Joe was asleep, until he smoothed my hair back.

"Did you really kiss me back that night?" I blurted out before I could stop the verbal diarrhea from spewing out. Old habits die hard.

"Mmmm hmmm," Joe said.

The old me would have asked nineteen questions. Why did he kiss me back? Did it mean he liked me? Did he want to be my boyfriend? How was the kiss? And on and on and on, but I decided, for once in my life, to just be content in a nice moment.

"That's good," I whispered and drifted off to sleep.

Jordana came in and discreetly shook me awake, glancing at Joe with a knowing smile. "Oh, Dr. Twelve Steps," she said, to which he awakened and stretched with a low lion roar.

"What time is it?" I asked her.

"Five thirty. I'm going to the reservoir. Tito wrote back. His cousin is trying to figure out the plan for this evening. Let's reconvene for breakfast at Sarabeth's below the park at seven?"

171

"Sounds good."

As Jordana walked out the door Joe reached down and intertwined his fingers with mine.

"I bought the Dixie Chicks album after you crashed that first AA meeting in the Presbyterian church."

"Did you like it?"

"No, it was terrible, awful, whiny stuff, but it made me smile when I listened to it because it reminded me of the madcap story you told that night. And it reminded me of you."

"Did you also buy *Downton Abbey*?"

He looked away. "I did."

"And?"

"It was pretty fantastic. I can't blame you on that front. I don't know if Lady Mary and Matthew Crawley are going to be able to make it work, but I'm rooting for them. Of course, that reminded me of you too. The entire twenty-one hours of it."

This was quite possibly the sweetest, nonforced thing a man had ever said to me. I decided I needed to return the favor with some memories of my own.

"You had Boston cream all over your face the night we met."

"Did I?"

"Yup. It was there forever. And Boston cream is my favorite."

"You could have told me."

"You looked cute with it on there."

And then he leaned down. It was definitely him who did the leaning this time and lightly brushed his lips over mine. This time I wasn't half in the bag and I was able to enjoy every second of his lips pushing down soft, and then harder. His hands came to the sides of my face as he slowly pulled back.

"Wow," I said.

"Wow back."

"If you're still not ready for a relationship, I totally understand."

"I am starting to think I'm ready."

"Oh good, because I think I'm ready."

I was ready for quite a lot actually and I think Joe was too, but we couldn't be ready just then since I could hear everyone else start to stir and groan their own morning sighs.

"To be continued?" I asked.

"Definitely."

We hastily untangled ourselves. I rallied the troops and got us all dressed and out the door. My favorite doorman, Nico, stopped me as I headed out and handed me a giant stack of mail.

"I weeded out all the crap, ma'am," he said with a wink. I stuffed it into my already overflowing purse and hailed us four cabs on Twenty-Third Street.

At Sarabeth's, Jordana informed us that she met her client exactly as planned and the client was so excited to see her (since Jordana had been conspicuously absent from the city), she insisted on having coffee and croissants, so Jordana had plenty of time to pump her for information. The tulip ceremony was indeed being broadcast live from the roof of the Empire State Building. They would begin setting up at 3:00 p.m. for a taping at 8:00 p.m. It would go down only slightly differently than Joe had explained. The Husband would meet the two women on the observation deck. He would pull one to the side to dump her before getting down on one knee to propose to the other one. The deck would be divided by a false wall so that the women weren't standing right next to each other.

The producer made our lives one hundred times easier when she offered Jordana tickets to the finale. There had been risers constructed for a live studio audience of about three hundred. In exchange, Jordana had to promise to come back to the city to give the producer three private yoga lessons. No one gives anyone anything for free in this town.

So we had tickets to the actual show and would at least be on deck if we couldn't stop whatever Stella was planning before this thing actually went on the air. Tito's cousin said he could sneak some of us onto the setup if we could find a pair of Carrefour coveralls to blend in with the workers. Tito was on his way into the city, and he said he and Princess would do just that to see if Stella had staked out the show early.

Joe had to drive the geriatrics van back to Yardville, since the hospital would soon be missing it, and then take a train back to the city to be there in time for the show.

I went back to my apartment with Annie and had lain down on the bed for a much needed nap when I heard, "I would do anything for love . . . but I won't do that." I glanced down at the phone's screen to see, "DO NOT CALL THIS LYING CHEATING BASTARD." It was Eric.

Annie rolled onto her side and saw the name flash across the screen just as I did.

"Don't answer it, Sophie."

"I wasn't going to."

"Seriously. I think you could have something great with Joe. He really likes you."

"How do you know?"

"I lied to you when you asked me before if he talked about you. He only talks about you *all* the time in my counseling sessions. He's lucky I quite like you myself or I would have told him to shut the hell up by now."

Butterflies began banging about in my belly again and a grin that I knew could only be described as goofy spread across my face. It occurred to me for a second how it was so odd that the belly could be the indicator of both extreme excitement and extreme grief. The butterflies and the rubber band of despair both resided in there, and both reacted to my sadness and happiness by clanging around. I wondered if one day they would ever have a showdown, and who would win. I wanted the butterflies to take the rubber band out for good.

"He likes me."

"He likes you. DFIU."

"Deefoo?"

"Don't fuck it up!"

Annie went out in search of more coffee and I hopped in the shower. When I emerged, there were six text messages from Eric.

I need to talk to you.

Please call.

I'm sorry, Sophie.

I made a huge mistake.

Will you please call me.

PLEASE.

Eric was never big on saying please, probably because he was so used to getting exactly what he wanted that he never had to.

What if I called him? What if I finally got the closure I needed? Besides, Step 8 was very clearly to make a list of all the persons we had harmed and make amends. Eric had harmed me, but I had definitely harmed him too, with my psychotic behavior following our breakup, so maybe it was time for me to make amends. Maybe that was how I could get the rubber band with Eric's name on it to go away once and for all.

He answered on the first ring.

"Thank you for calling. Seriously, thank you, Sophie."

"Congratulations, Eric. Megan told me the news, and I hope you two have a wonderful wedding."

"There isn't going to be a wedding. Lacey left me last night."

This was not what I was expecting. Not in a million years did I think someone like Lacey would ever leave someone like Eric, but then I thought twice and couldn't think of any redeeming qualities Eric really had to hang on to anyone, even someone I didn't have a terrible amount of respect for. Even someone like Lacey. Ooooo, I was calling her Lacey and not Floozy. This was a healing moment. Oh gosh, and it had been weeks since I looked at a single tweet she had written. In fact, I had been so good about ignoring the both of them on all forms of social media that I was genuinely blindsided by Eric's news. I'd have to remember to pat myself on the back later. Progress!

"Can I see you?"

"I don't know if that's a good idea."

"I just want to talk to you. I think we have things we both need to say."

He was right, and I had never been able to say no to that man. I agreed that I would stop by his apartment on my way to meet Jordana, Annie, and Joe at the show. It was time for both of us to make some amends.

Make amends whenever possible, except when doing so might cause someone harm

Eric lived in one of those imposing Upper East Side buildings with four doormen who gave you the judgy face when you came over looking anything less than perfect, which was pretty much me all the time. The front desk guy, who I called Dragon because of his long red ponytail, was ready for my arrival this time and buzzed me right up to the penthouse with nary a judgy stare.

Eric's door was cracked, and he was sitting, back facing me, front to the floor-to-ceiling windows that overlooked Midtown—including the Empire State Building.

He turned around to reveal puffy eyes, a stained T-shirt, and at least two days' worth of a beard. I had never seen him anything but entirely clean-shaven and perfect looking. He prided himself on his utter perfectness. I almost laughed before catching myself and realizing this would be the absolute worst thing I could do. Besides, he looked exactly like me when I was padding around Grandma's house in my velour jammies right after our breakup. There was something comforting in that fact.

He slowly stood and padded barefoot to meet me, wrapping his arms around my shoulders and resting his chin on my head.

"It feels like shit."

"What feels like shit, Eric?"

"Getting dumped. Now I know what I put you through."

"Is that why you called? To tell me you understood what I went through?"

Now I was starting to get angry. I didn't want his sympathy. I pulled back.

"Eric, you don't know what I went through. You and Floo—Lacey have been together what? Three months? We dated for two years. You met my parents. I met your parents. We took vacations together. We talked about getting married. It's a little different."

But was it different? Who was I to say how in love or in lust with Lacey he actually was? Maybe he had imagined a whole future with her the way I had imagined it with him. I made a silent vow to be more patient and to listen to what he had to say.

For his part, Eric genuinely seemed unable to comprehend why I couldn't understand his newfound pain. Then it clicked for me: He wanted a tribe, and I was the nearest thing he could make an emotional connection with. Eric had no siblings. His family was as WASPy as they came and firmly eschewed the F word—feelings. I really was all that he had. I was his emotional wastebasket. He wanted to have a pity party and I was the only person he knew to invite.

That pissed me off. "I'm not your shoulder to cry on. You gave that up when you broke up with me. I hate you, remember? Or I hat*ed* you. I hated you that night I put your penis on the Internet, and I think maybe I even still hated you last night. Last night I thought about naming my boat after . . . never mind. But now I don't hate you. Right in this moment, I think I have finally stopped hating you. Now I feel sorry for you. Now I want you to move on, not from me, but from Floozy. Live your life without a woman to lean on for once in your life, Eric."

"Did you meet someone else?"

I sighed. "Eric, no. Maybe. I don't know. I'm not dating anyone else, and unlike you, I am certainly not sleeping with anyone else. But that is none of your business. Come on, Eric. Let's be grown-ups now."

He sank back into his chair to pout. Eric wasn't going to be a grown-up anytime soon. But I had to be. I had a televised proposal to crash on the roof of the Empire State Building in less than an hour.

"Eric, I'm using the bathroom." He just nodded.

I walked into his stately marble washroom and laughed when I saw the carefully arrayed bottles of skin moisturizer and conditioner. Eric definitely needed a tribe, if only to talk to about his beauty regimen. As I washed my hands I took a look at my watch. SHIT. I seriously had less than forty-five minutes to get to Midtown. I ran out of the bathroom and grabbed my iPhone off Eric's kitchen counter. Then I walked over to his chair where he hadn't moved an inch. I leaned down and kissed him on the cheek. "You're gonna be OK, buddy. I promise." I really thought he would. Eric is the kind of guy who will always land on his feet somehow. And even when you hope for the worst, it just isn't going to happen to him. Had those penis pictures somehow leaked onto the real Internet, he probably would have gotten offered a job as a penis stunt double or something. For some people things always turn up roses.

Of course, because I was in a rush there were no cabs. I hopped into one of the black gypsy cabs before realizing that I had no money.

"Shit! Shit! . . . I'm sorry, sir, I have no cash."

"Then you leave my cab."

"But I really need to get to the Empire State Building. We can maybe stop at an ATM."

"No, no, you get out of my cab." With that he pulled over onto Park Avenue and made it abundantly clear that I was to exit the vehicle. OK. Subway. I ran to the nearest entrance and fifteen minutes later was huffing and puffing my way into our designated meeting spot in the Heartland Brewery at Thirty-Fifth Street. I ran smack into Joe.

"Hey, you. We were starting to get worried." His eyes were filled with so much affection that for a moment I considered not telling him that I had been with Eric for the past hour, but then I decided that I didn't want to start a relationship with anything but total honesty.

"I'm sorry. I was . . ."

"SOPHIE!" Jordana interrupted before I could get it out. "We still haven't located her. We have to go to Plan B."

Plan B was to call Jordana's producer friend and alert her to the situation. The last thing Stella needed was to embarrass herself on national television.

I sighed. "I agree." Jordana went out onto the street to make the call, brushing past Princess and Tito, who ran in breathless. I looked over at them, and they just shook their heads. No luck. I was again about to tell Joe about my afternoon but when Princess is around, it can be hard to get a word in edgewise, and after only five minutes, Jordana came back in, her face grim.

"What's up?" I asked.

"Well, I told the producer everything. I told her that Stella was probably planning to crash the wedding and that they should take extra precaution and maybe even shut down the filming. And she asked me for a description of her, so I sent her a picture. And then I asked what she would do and she told me nothing. She laughed like a maniac and said she thought this would give the show the highest ratings it has had in years."

"Shit!"

"OK, well, we have to get up there. Maybe we can minimize the damage somehow." The streets around the giant skyscraper were blocked off and we had to show our IDs to the guards at the bottom as well as the e-mailed confirmation from Jordana's producer friend that we all had seats to the show.

It was a modern-day Coliseum on the roof. Bleacher seats

surrounded an interior stage with a grand marble slab divided by a wall. On each side there was a podium with a red velvet ring box perched on top. Of course, we all knew only one of those boxes contained a ring. Flatscreens surrounded the setup so that no one would miss any of the bloody action on either side. Instead of sacrificing Christians to the lions, we were watching single women have their hearts broken for entertainment.

The bleachers were packed, and the desperation in the air was palpable. The host, Danny McMasters, a former child star turned meth addict turned born-again Christian turned reality television hotshot, strolled the set in his pin-striped three-piece suit sans tie. Still no sign of Stella anywhere. The introduction music began to crescendo and McMasters received his final primping, a spritz with an airbrush gun of concealer and some superhold hairspray to ensure his hair never moved an inch against the gusty winds 102 stories above Midtown Manhattan—and we were off. A live television bloodbath was about to begin.

When we are wrong, promptly admit it

"What you are about to see here tonight will be the most excit-ing *Husband* finale yet," Danny McMasters boomed from center stage. "We've all watched as Jake has met and gotten to know twenty-seven beautiful women, and whittled them down to the two here tonight. They have had intimate moments. There have been tears. They have met each other's families, and tonight, Jake will reveal which of these women is his soul mate." I heard Annie snort at the mention of soul mate. "One woman will go home to plan her wedding, and the other will nurse her broken heart. In just an hour we will know which one is which. But first let's take a look back at how Jake's relationships with Erika and Kimberly have progressed."

Cue "From This Moment On" by Shania Twain and a three-minute montage of Jake's relationships with two women. First the meeting where the women step out of a black limousine in their too-tiny dresses and towering heels and try to say something funny to get Jake's attention so he'll remember them fondly at the end of the night when he doles out his first round of tulips. Erika spoke to Jake in his mom's native tongue, Dutch. Kimberly did a backflip upon exiting the limo.

Then their one-on-one dates, where they sip champagne and try to reveal their entire life stories in just a couple of hours while cameras keep zooming in for their close-ups. Then the exotic tropical date where Jake gets to ask each woman if they want to spend the night in the fantasy suite. There's Jake looking like the prizewinning pig at the State Fair in a hot tub with Erika, kissing on the beach with Kimberly. Then the visits to the families where Jake promises each woman's parents that he is falling in love with their daughter. Erika's Texan father is understandably skeptical.

"Don't you break my little girl's heart, Jake," Daddy said as he cocked a shotgun.

And then the screens went dark. In fact, the entire area went dark. And as if by magic, Erika and Kimberly were now on their separate sides of the stage, each attired in a white minidress that I assumed was supposed to signify the possibility that one of them would be one step closer to marriage at the end of the night.

Taking a closer look, I realized that bachelorette number two was not Kimberly at all. It was Stella, resplendent in a white minidress, her hair done in a perfect chignon, green eyes gleaming.

The producers must have realized it at the same time I did; I could hear Jordana's client hiss, "Keep going. Just keep going. We're live!" The rest of the audience, expecting twists and turns from their reality programming, was ready to go with the flow and watch to see what would happen. I dug my nails into Joe's arm.

"What's she going to do?"

"I don't know, but you have to give her props for getting this far," Joe stage-whispered to me.

Jake strolled onstage next to McMasters, oblivious that his moment to shine was about to be shut down by an ex-girlfriend on a rampage.

"Jake, it's been a long ride, hasn't it?" McMasters asked.

Jake nodded earnestly as if he had just come back from war instead of making out with twenty-seven women.

"Tonight is the big night. Tonight you choose your wife, Jake. Are you ready?"

"I am, Danny. I really am." At that, Jake lowered his head just slightly and gave a coy smile to the women in the live studio audience, proving that Jake was nowhere near ready for anything resembling monogamy.

"One of these women will be leaving here with a broken heart tonight, Jake. You know how this works. I need you to break up with one of the women gently before you can propose to your one true love."

Jake reached his hand up to his face as if to brush away an imaginary tear.

McMasters put a brotherly arm around Jake's shoulder and

steered him toward the two women. Which way would he turn? Would it be better for him to "dump" Stella first?

But no. Jake headed in the direction of Erika, and the crowd gave a collective gasp. He walked through the soundproof door. For a moment her face lit up. Poor Erika didn't know she was first. I noticed her dad in the audience straighten up a little. I wondered if security here was good enough to find concealed firearms. She reached out her arms to Jake in what might have been one of the saddest gestures I had ever seen. You might expect him to give her a signal, a slight shake of his head, a wink—anything so that she didn't have to experience this breakup in real time in front of a live studio audience and millions of viewers around the world.

Tears of joy (not for long) glistened in her eyes. Jake took her in his arms, looked down into her heart-shaped face, and sighed. It was the sigh of a winner, the sigh of the one who was doing the dumping. It was a self-satisfied sigh all of us, save for some very lucky supermodels like Heidi Klum or perhaps Kate Moss, have heard at one point in our lives. But Erika must not have heard the sigh before. She was young, like, twenty-three, and pretty. It's entirely possible she had never been sighed at in such a manner, since the glow of expectancy hadn't yet fallen from her face.

"Erika."

"Jake."

"The time we have spent together has been so special."

"It has, hasn't it."

Oh no. She really had never been dumped before; she didn't understand any of the dumping subtext. This *was* like watching a lamb thrown to the lions.

"But," and on the *but*, I think she knew, like any human being has the instinct to recognize when something is going bad, when they've failed a test or their parents are about to tell them they're getting a divorce. That *but* changed things.

"But?" she stuttered.

"But I am in love with someone else." Off to stage left McMasters now pretended to wipe his own single tear from his cheek.

"But you met my parents. You said you were falling in love with me. You didn't mean any of it?"

"I did. I really, really did. It's just that I felt something more for Kimberly." Now Erika was a full-blown waterworks, tears streaming down her cheeks, her face getting red and blotchy. She was an ugly crier, and you could tell Jake was ready to get away from her. He began shifting his feet back and forth like he had to pee. At this point, in the real world, something would happen. The guy would begin inching toward the door, the girl would begin throwing things (the producers carefully kept nothing within arm's reach), or worse, she would throw herself at him in a pitiful bid to use sex as a weapon to keep things going just a little while longer. But only thirty minutes were left in the show, and Erika couldn't be left blubbering onstage. This was McMasters's cue. He swooped in to put his arm around the sobbing girl. But Erika wasn't giving up without a fight.

"I gave you a blow job in the fantasy suite!" she screamed.

Producers frantically began trying to bleep her out. "Blow job" was not family-friendly conversation for prime time, but being so jazzed over the concept of a live breakup, they hadn't thought to put in a delay, so Erika's words reached the ears of small children across the land watching *The Husband* with their moms. "You said I had to SHOW you I loved you. I SHOWED you. I SHOWED you for an hour. An HOUR. Who takes an hour?" At this point, the producers seemed to have things under control and McMasters had managed to pull away back to stage left. The camera panned to him, and he immediately plastered on his saccharine sweet smile.

"That was a doozy, huh, folks."

Behind him it was obvious that Erika was still railing on Jake, but their mics had been silenced.

"Let's give these former lovebirds some time during a commercial break, brought to you by our sponsors, Durex condoms and Kay Jewelers, and then we'll come back for Jake's proposal." Of course, McMasters and everyone in the live audience knew that no proposal was going to happen because some strange broad had replaced Kimberly. At this point no one had any clue what to think. Not even us.

"We have to stop her now," I whispered to Joe. "We have to stop her before she makes a complete fool out of herself like Erika." As I said her name, Erika was being pulled from the stage kicking and screaming like a banshee.

"Check out that security, Sophie. We aren't getting through them." It was true; I hadn't noticed before, but the edge of the stage was lined with what looked like the starting lineup of the New Zealand rugby team, each one bigger than the next, in matching aviator sunglasses.

I harrumphed. "You'd think this was a presidential debate and not some silly reality television competition."

Joe laughed. "Is there really a difference between the two anymore?" He had a point.

With Erika safely offstage (hopefully sedated) and Jake given a pep talk like he was Rocky Balboa about to go for a final round against Apollo Creed, the lights on set began to flicker and the warning bell chimed that the commercial break was about to come to an end. There was McMasters explaining how Jake was about to propose to his one true love, his soul mate, his best friend. But at this point during the show, when the studio audience would usually be eating out of the palm of his hand, McMasters had to know something was a little off. For once, the audience was skeptical. The mirror had been broken, the pond rippled. Reality television had never felt so real.

"Jake, are you ready?"

What would Stella do? Would she claw him and scream at him the way Erika had? Would she reveal terrible and embarrassing things about him in front of the live audience?

"I'm ready, Danny." Jake turned and walked through door number two. At first he definitely didn't comprehend what was happening to him. There was a glimmer of recognition before a look of utter confusion came over his face. I dug my nails into Joe's forearm.

Stella, cool and collected, merely smiled.

"Hi, Jake."

McMasters knew his cue when he saw it. He strode over to Stella and put an arm around her waist.

"You are certainly not Kimberly, my dear. What happened to Kimberly?"

"Well, Danny," Stella replied in an equally measured and television-friendly tone, "it seems that maybe Kimberly wasn't as in love with Jake as Jake seems to have thought. I had a little chat with her before the show and she was having what you might call . . . cold feet. After talking to her for a while, she asked that I come in her place to tell Jake personally just how sorry she was that she couldn't go through with this."

"I see." McMasters rubbed his stubby chin with his stubby fingers. "And who, may I ask, are you?"

Stella smiled. "I'm Jake's ex-girlfriend, Stella."

"And why did you come here tonight, Stella?"

"For closure. I want to ask Jake one question, and then I want to move on."

Jake couldn't have looked more terrified. The studio audience members were on the edge of their seats, and Erika's wails could still slightly be heard from offstage. Behind me I heard Prithi make a low growl in anticipation.

"Why not me, Jake?" Three words that every woman wants to ask after a breakup but never has the courage to say out loud. Why not me? We don't really want to know the answer to that question. We don't want to hear that we actually weren't pretty enough or young enough or smart enough or good enough in the bedroom or that his mom secretly didn't want him to marry us because of the time she caught you giving him a hand job under the holiday table. We don't want to know that his friends thought our laugh was annoying or that since we began dating our tummies had gotten too soft for his liking. We don't want to know the answer to this question, but we *have* to know it. Not knowing is what keeps us from moving on. If we don't hear the horrible truth, we can cling to some small shred of hope that we might still have a chance.

That's when Jake surprised us all by completely going off script, his personal script, the measured one he probably always stuck to because he was that kind of guy who always planned everything in advance. . . . He was honest.

"Look. I couldn't imagine you being the last one. I just couldn't. And then here I was with twenty-seven women, thinking, 'Whoooa, I have twenty-seven women, one of them will be the last one.' And it was the same thing all over again. I'm not ready for the last one."

Stella stared at him, a surprising lack of anger in her eyes; instead, it had been replaced with something that almost looked like pity and resignation. She walked over toward Jake and put her hand on his arm; he flinched visibly.

"OK," she said. It was that simple. Just an OK. The meetings, the steps, the silence even—all of it had worked for Stella.

And then Prithi groaned. I thought what Stella said was great, how she acted was great; what problem could Prithi possibly have with it? And then she groaned again deeper this time and grabbed my shoulder.

"Sophie . . . I think the baby's coming."

I squawked and full bansheed out of my seat, ignoring all regulations that the studio audience remain silent save for claps, cheers, sighs, and measured sniffling. Stella looked over, Jake continued to look confused, and McMasters's expression didn't alter even a wee bit. Botox must be a wonderful thing.

Prithi stood up, leaving a puddle on her seat. Joe wrapped his arm around her.

"Stay calm, Prith. We're in New York. There are a dozen hospitals within walking distance. We're going to get you in a cab, and everything is going to be OK."

Joe looked at me. "Sophie, give me your phone so I can call my friend at NYU and let him know we're on our way stat." I dug my iPhone out of my bag and handed it to Joe, then began clearing an aisle for Prithi to walk down to get the heck out of the audience. The cameras continued to roll on our drama, being live television and all. McMasters for once seemed to be at a loss for words. I waved awkwardly to the camera. "Hi, Mom."

Our mad entourage made it into the elevator and downstairs. As I settled Prithi into the back of a cab, Joe slid into the backseat next to me.

"We're all set. My friend Dr. Uluhru will meet us at NYU; everything is going to be OK, Prithi." Then in Joe's hand I saw my cell phone begin to ring.

"The doctor must be calling me back," Joe said. Except my phone wasn't ringing Meatloaf; it was ringing a more distinctive ring that I knew just as well. It was ringing "I'm Bringing Sexy Back" and I caught a fleeting glimpse of the screen as Joe raised it to his ear and answered; my stomach tightened into a knot as I read "Crazy Fucking Bitch" light up the place on the screen where a name should have appeared.

It wasn't my phone. But I was apparently the crazy fucking bitch in question, the same way Eric was "Do Not Call That Lying Cheating Bastard."

"Hey, Dr. Uluhru. We're on our way." Joe looked at me and smiled.

"Sophie? You want to talk to Sophie? Who is this? Eric?" I saw confusion, then recognition wash over Joe's face. "Sophie left her phone at your apartment this afternoon? OK. Of course, here she is." He turned to me, his face stone cold.

"It's for you." I tried to plead with Joe with my eyes for sympathy, for a break, for anything, but he had already looked away and was calming Prithi and telling the driver where to go over her grunts and moans.

"Hi, Eric . . . yeah, I think I grabbed your phone. I am going to NYU. No, I'm fine. Want to meet me in the emergency room and we can switch? OK, sounds good."

I hung up. "Joe, I can explain."

"No need. I guess you were busy this afternoon. It's fine. It's totally fine. I am fine with this. Fine."

Prithi looked from one of us to the other like we were crazy.

Joe turned all his attention on her. I was very obviously not a priority for him.

"Breathe, Prithi. I need you to just breathe."

"I'm sorry," I whispered.

He didn't answer. His therapist bedside manner was firmly intact.

I tried to breathe.

Listen to that higher power (whoever she may be). She knows her shit.

Only two people were allowed in the delivery room with Prithi, so I waited outside while Joe and Sasank coached her through the rest of her labor. The other ladies, who had met us at the hospital, grabbed taxis back to my apartment to get a couple of hours of rest, but I felt obligated to stay, both for Prithi and for Joe, just to let him know I wasn't going anywhere.

With nothing else to do after having read a three-week-old *US Weekly* twice, I decided to tackle the mail. Nico really had weeded out all the crap. He left the copies of *Real Simple* and removed the *New Yorker*, which he must have somehow guessed always just collected dust in my bathroom. I paid all my bills online so there were none of those.

At the bottom of the stack was a hot pink envelope. No one

sent me letters anymore! Maybe it was a reminder from my gynecologist to schedule my yearly pap smear?

As I looked closer I recognized my grandmother's signature cursive handwriting. The postmark was dated a week before she died. My heart skipped a beat as I slid my finger beneath the flap and opened this missive from beyond the grave. It was a card, not a letter. On the front was a giant sparkly diamond. On the inside was a picture of delicious-looking chocolate cake. Above it were the words: *Meet your real best friend.* Eleanor had taken up the entire left panel of the card, the bottom half of the right, and then continued on a piece of her hand-bordered Crane stationery.

Dear Sophie,

Hi, beautiful girl!

First, I want to tell you I am going to miss your face a ton and a bushel and a peck when I am gone.

That's why I am writing this. I know that pretty soon I won't be around and I just wanted to send you one last note that will make you smile. I also want to impart some end of the road wisdom when you can't get mad at me anymore, either because I'm no longer here or because I am a sick and frail old woman who shouldn't be trifled with.

YOU SHOULD NOT SETTLE FOR THAT MANNEQUIN, MOISTURIZING PRETTY BOY you've been toying around with. He doesn't make you happy. In fact, I still don't think you

*know who or what will make you happy. That's what you need
to figure out, beautiful girl. What do you want?*

*For a long time I didn't know what I wanted. I knew
that I didn't want your grandfather. That snake in the grass
cheated on me with every secretary from here to Tulsa.
When he finally had that heart attack (on top of a typist
in Denver I might add), I was finally ready to start my life.
That's when I decided to figure out what I wanted . . . and to
ask for it. So at that point in my life I wanted to be adored.
And I wanted to have great sex. Once I knew that is what I
wanted I was able to go out and get it. You want to be loved,
but you don't know how that will work since you don't really love yourself that much right now. I LOVE YOU. YOU
SHOULD LOVE YOU. And some man out there should love
you and adore you and worship the ground you walk on.
Once you think you've found that man, tell him that's what
you want from him. If he is the right guy, then he will give
you exactly that.*

You deserve only everything.

Love,

Eleanor

*PS—Watch out for Enrique's grandson. He seems like a
handful.*

Tears streamed down my face as I read and reread the note.

My grandfather was a man-whore. That was an uncomfortable
fact to absorb, but somehow made me feel better. Eleanor didn't

have the perfect love either. That shook my worldview. I had always envied her having that one, great love. Now that I knew her love wasn't all that great, all that was left to envy was her ability to know exactly what she wanted and then ask for it. She—not any man—controlled her happiness.

I was finally strong enough to try to control my own.

Joseph Sasank Biswas Mehti was born at 1:00 a.m. weighing seven pounds, two ounces. Sasank's boyfriend, Michael, and all the ladies from the house returned to the hospital, of course, to welcome him into the world.

Sasank called the baby's father to tell him the news. It went straight to voice mail. Prithi seemed unfazed. Stella joined us at the hospital when the show was over. At first she was hangdog and apologetic.

"It was like the last step for me, you know?" she said. We did know, and we all told her that we understood. She did what she needed to do. Even Katrina was forgiving about the stolen Louboutins.

"Keep them, love," she told Stella. "Now they're famous."

Twitter and Facebook had gone off the hook for Stella. This *Husband* finale had received more tweets than all the past finales combined, and #StellaRocks and #YouTellHimStella both trended before the broadcast was over.

And more than that, the producers of *The Husband* loved Stella so much they asked her to come back for the next season as *The Wife*. She was still thinking it over. McMasters had apparently given her a ride to the hospital, with his hand on her knee the entire time he was making the pitch.

I hardly saw Joe throughout Prithi's four hours of labor. The doctor allowed him in the delivery room in lieu of a husband, so he had helped to coach Prithi through the birth. My nails bitten to the quick, I had finally grabbed Annie just before midnight.

"I saw Eric today."

She groaned.

"Gross, why?"

"He called. I needed the closure. I needed what Stella got."

"And did you get it?"

"I did. It felt great. I felt nothing. I actually just felt good."

Annie hugged me.

"Well then, good, Soph. I'm proud of you."

"But."

"I swear if I hear one more *but* today I am going to lose it."

"But I left my phone there and then I grabbed his phone by accident and then he called my phone, no, his phone, and Joe answered it and it was Eric and now he hates me."

"Why would he hate you for that?"

"Because we kissed this morning and because his ex-wife cheated on him and he found out by answering her phone and he might not even be ready for a relationship, but if he was, then this might be enough to make him not be ready."

"Have you explained what happened to him?"

"I couldn't. Prithi was in labor and then we were in a cab and now she's having a baby and I am biting my nails and I don't know what to do."

"You know, Sophie. You should go for a walk. Think about what you even want from Joe. Think about if you're ready. You might not be and that's OK. You told us all that part of your problem is that you love being in love. Maybe that means you need to take things extra slow from now on."

She was right. I hugged her and walked out the hospital doors. I walked through Times Square, just as crowded during the night as it was during the day, maybe more so. I saw snippets of *The Husband* being played on the Jumbotron on Forty-Third Street.

I didn't love Eric anymore. I probably never *really* loved Eric. I was infatuated with him and I loved the idea of him, in all his seeming perfect-for-the-future-ness, but I never loved him as a person. Now that I had finally let him go, his person was actually a little stomach-turning to me. Looking back, I had loved the idea of all my boyfriends, had loved the idea of being in love, but I hadn't truly been in love with them. I wanted them to turn me and my life into what I imagined it should be. Being in love should be a selfless act, where you do something for the other person, where it isn't about you anymore, where you surrender what you want for the good of the pair, or sometimes for the good of one, the one who isn't you.

I returned to the hospital with puffy eyes. Our entire little group, our motley family of addicts of both substance and emotion, was cooing over the one great thing to come out of a very bad relationship.

I went to the handicapped bathroom to wash my face and try to regain some outward signs of dignity. Of course, the hospital bathroom only had air dryers and no paper towels. After trying to dab the moisture off with toilet paper, I resigned myself to doing a backbend in front of the blower and letting the whoosh of air dry my face.

While I was reapplying makeup there was a knock on the door.

"Hold on a sec," I yelled.

"Soph?"

It was Joe.

"Yeah, it's me," I mumbled weakly.

"Can I come in for a second?" I had only applied eyeliner and mascara on one eye and looked vaguely like the comic villain Two-Face.

I cracked the door the width of a body to seem inconspicuous, and he slid through sideways. He looked so tired, but softer, less angry, more open to what I had to say.

My eyes welled up with tears again sending the non-waterproof liner running in a jagged stream down my left cheek.

"I only have makeup on one eye."

"I can see that," he said, with just the hint of a smile. "You still look beautiful." He paused. "Sophie, there's something I need to tell you . . ."

I took a deep breath and closed both eyes. "Me first. Please. We're not ready for this," I said with much more conviction than I thought I was going to be able to bring to this talk. Before he could talk, I kept going on. "You need to finish working on you.

You need to become a doctor again. I need to finish working on me and not let my next relationship sweep me back into a cycle of craziness. You are amazing and awesome and I have to admit that in the past twenty-four hours—hell, before the last twenty-four hours—I already broke the rule I created and started picturing the two of us walking down an aisle, having three babies, and moving into my grandmother's house, but that's why I need to take a step back. I don't want to repeat the same mistakes.

"If we do this, if you ever want to do this—and after all this, you probably don't and that will be fine and I will never publish nude photos of you on the Internet—but if we do, then I want to start clean and fresh and healthy."

He just looked at me and wrapped his arms around my waist. Then Joe kissed me very lightly on the mouth. It was great, which is all there is to say about it. Then he turned around and slid back out the door the same way he had come in.

I sank down on the closed toilet seat and waited for the tears to come again.

But they had stopped.

For the first time in a very long time I felt right.

Having had a spiritual awakening, carry our message to others

Six Months Later

"Do you have an extra bathing suit I could borrow?"

"We're not the same size, Annie. You have enormous boobs."

"I just need the bottom. I'm going topless in Mexico."

Of course she was. Annie off the sauce was exactly like Annie on the sauce, except sometimes more polite and at least 90 percent less likely to steal cars. She had taken the train into Manhattan to see me. Soon after *The Husband* and Prithi's big day, my editor had demanded I return to be on call for the final publishing schedule of our next release.

Megan and I were was also in preliminary talks about turning the makeshift rules and steps we had created for LAA into a self-help book. She thought she could get Suze to write the introduction.

That meant I hadn't seen or spoken to Joe in six months. He

took my words to heart and had maybe even decided he didn't want anything to do with me after all.

And that was OK.

The LAA meetings continued but turned more into social events. We coached Stella on her new gig as "the Wife;" we took little Joey to the park. Prithi decided to scrap med school. She couldn't keep living her parents' American dream. She was living hers and Joey's. For now, they were living in Eleanor's house, which remained on the market, and Prithi took care of the place while I was back in my old apartment. Annie came to stay with me most weekends, now that working at the bar was less appealing. She was thinking about opening an Indian fusion restaurant with Prithi and had a hot new investment banker girlfriend who was willing to front some cash for it. Dave had been in an actual functioning relationship with an accountant named Mandy for almost four months. He had yet to call her a turkey.

I had even gone on a few dates. One was a set-up through Megan: the grandson of one of her Tomatoes. He was a really nice architect who lived in Gramercy and had an adorable roly-poly black lab. Not once did I picture myself walking down the aisle with him. I was just letting myself have fun and enjoying hanging out with someone new. I didn't know if it would go anywhere and that was fine with me.

The only member of our group we hadn't seen or heard from in a few months was Katrina, whom we assumed had gone off retreating somewhere, until a letter arrived two weeks ago.

Before I opened it Annie asked, "Have you seen Tito lately?"

"No, I haven't been back to the house. My publisher has had me working every single weekend. Why, does the lawn look like shit?"

"No, it looks as good as it always does, but Tito's guys have been working on it, not Tito."

"That's weird. I can call him or maybe Katrina knows where he is. They were really friendly back at the house."

"*Really* friendly," Annie said with a smile, throwing a gold-embossed piece of tissue paper on my couch.

Mr. and Mrs. Melberg are pleased to invite you to the wedding of their daughter Katrina to Mr. Tito Juarez III, at his family estate in Puerto Morelos, Mexico.

"Tito has a family estate?"

"More like, Tito is marrying Princess?" Annie yelled.

But it made sense. Love Addicts Anonymous had taught Princess to break her cycle of dating closeted Jewish mama's boys just because they were Jewish and fawned all over her, fulfilling the idea of some imaginary perfect man that she had kept in her head since the first time she imagined Cinderella and Snow White beginning their happily ever afters under a chuppah. Tito was so outside her wheelhouse she never would have looked at him twice unless she was put in a basement and forced to do karaoke with him on a weekly basis. Even then, if she hadn't confronted and broken her cycle of falling for men who were never going to love her back, she wouldn't have been able to realize that someone like Tito was someone she wanted.

I leaped up and down and clapped my hands like a five-year-old handed a Pixy Stix, or one of those *Toddlers & Tiaras* girls getting their second Red Bull. "I love this. Let's book tickets." We talked to the other girls in the group. Everyone had their tickets booked already, but Jordana was able to use her miles to get both Annie and me a good fare.

I used Rent-the-Runway to procure a very sexy, hot pink Herve Leger bandage dress.

It wasn't until we got on the plane that the obvious occurred to me.

"Joe will be there."

"That's likely," Annie said. She had continued to talk to Joe on a fairly regular basis but was careful not to let her relationship with him bleed into her relationship with me after I told her what happened in that hospital bathroom.

"So he will be there?"

"Yes, Sophie."

"Is he bringing anyone?"

"I honestly don't know. He had talked about trying to book a ticket at one point and he said he was having passport problems. I would tell you more if I knew."

I said a silent serenity prayer. I may have been a recovering love addict, but that didn't mean I was entirely cured.

Puerto Morelos is twenty miles south of Cancun and worlds away from the place where I got a rash during high school Senior Week after a very unfortunate foam party at a place called Coco

Bongo. The beaches were pearly white, the water a perfect turquoise, and Tito's family estate was . . . HUGE. It was a giant gated compound outside of town with about three entrances and four kilometers of uninterrupted beach all to itself.

"Why was Tito our gardener again?" I asked Annie.

"I think he couldn't get a proper work visa to do anything else, and he and his dad liked being in America better than Mexico."

"Do you think Katrina knew about this when she said she would marry him?"

Annie shrugged. I would later find out that Katrina hadn't known anything about Tito's secret monetary wealth until one night three months ago when he took her to the Botanical Gardens in Brooklyn and pulled a Spanish guitar from behind a stately maple tree.

"I wrote this song when I was seventeen years old," he said to her, strumming a Latin tune. "I wrote it about a brown-haired girl who showed me that the world I knew was only a small part of the world and how I wanted to spend my life traveling that unknown world with her."

As you can imagine, at this point for Katrina it was waterworks central and she was barely able to get her yes out in between her sobs. No man had ever treated her like such a woman, a woman who wasn't his mother, an object of absolutely pure desire.

They were later arrested for public indecency in an azalea bush.

We were immediately handed mojitos—virgin for Annie—as we walked into the open air receiving area at the main house.

Princess came barreling toward us in a strapless white Alice and Olivia dress and a diamond-studded tiara, nearly knocking Annie over with her hug.

"I'm getting married!" she squealed.

We squealed back!

"This place is amazing, Katrina," I said, still taking it all in.

"You haven't seen the best part yet." She smiled slyly. "Follow me."

We walked through some of the nicest gardens I had ever seen and down a beach past crystal-clear cerulean water. Katrina was leading us to a group of villas about a football field's length from the main house. We walked through a gate and into another receiving area.

"Welcome to love rehab!" Katrina squealed yet again.

"Ha, ha, yeah, of course. We will all be reunited here for the first time since we left one another at my house," I said.

"No," Katrina said. "Welcome to Love Rehab. This is the new love retreat!"

"What are you talking about?"

"Sophie, your idea was brilliant. Women, and even men, need what you created. It changed my life. Tito agrees, and he gave me this part of the estate for Love Rehab. Twice a year we will host the love retreat here. Maximum fifteen people per retreat. Meetings, yoga, karaoke nights, two weeks long. We can really help people."

I was speechless. It was brilliant. It was something only Princess could have pulled off.

"Twice a year?"

"Yup, twice a year. You'll come down to run the meetings.

Jordana will do yoga. Prithi will cook, and Joe will do the one-on-one counseling."

"Joe?"

"He's inside, Sophie."

"With his date?" I asked.

"He did bring someone."

I didn't know how to feel or react. I just nodded.

"He'll be at dinner, which—oy!—is in an hour. We have to get ready."

"Aren't you ready?"

"This is my day tiara."

Princess moved us back to the main house. I remained in a daze about Love Rehab and about Joe. Who could he have brought? Probably a lovely fellow doctor from the hospital.

Annie and I showered quickly and got ready. I invested a little more time than usual in my hair and makeup routine until Annie pulled me out to the dining room.

Joe was already at the table talking to a portly man with darker skin and a mustache, who I assumed was a relative of Tito's. Joe's date was nowhere in sight.

I sat down opposite him and a few seats down. He averted his eyes from his conversation companion, looked at me, and beamed.

"Hi, Sophie," he said with an undue amount of enthusiasm.

"Hi, Joe," I said almost shyly.

"It is so good to see you."

"You too." Joe's neighbor rose from his chair and walked out to the kitchen.

Then everyone was in the room. It was Jordana and Prithi and Olivia and Cameron and about a billion of Tito's and Princess's cousins and extended family members. Nothing is more chaotic than a Mexican-Jewish wedding. Princess had a seating plan, which actually put Joe and me at opposite ends of the table. His date never showed. Maybe she didn't feel well and was taking a nap or something.

As the dessert course was wheeled out on a giant cart I began to feel a little sleepy myself. I got up and walked to Katrina and whispered in her ear.

"I think I need to hit the sack early to be fresh for tomorrow," I said. She nodded and kissed my cheek, leaving a perfect heart-shaped mark with her MAC Viva Glam 5.

I walked out onto the beach to get some air and saw a jetty of rocks stretching into the black expanse. That looked relaxing, climbing out to the jetty, being able to hear the waves breaking on all sides of me. I took off my shoes, stacked them under a palm tree, and then carefully made my way out to the end. It was quite a long jetty, stretching the length of at least two city blocks into the ocean. I almost lost my balance a couple of times and was squarely out of breath by the time I reached the end. But I felt like I had accomplished something, and that's always a good feeling.

I also felt peaceful. Joe had looked happy, and for once in my life I just wanted the person I cared about to be happy, whether that was with or without me. For Joe it looked like it would be with the date he brought. And if she made him happy, I felt good. I sat down and rested my chin on my knees, enjoying the salty spray that came and cooled my face. Out of the corner of my eye, I thought I saw something fall right out of the sky. Then it happened again. And again. It was a flock of birds. Specifically, it was a flock of pelicans.

These were the birds Joe had told me about. They were falling to catch their fish. He was right; they seemed to give up flight completely as they hurtled into the sea, but each and every time they swooped back into the sky with their fish. They fell hard and got their fish each and every time. The birds entranced me. It must have been thirty or forty minutes I watched them before I realized that I had been gone quite a long time. I turned around, ready to go back, but I couldn't see the rocks any longer. In fact the only rocks between the shore and me were the ones directly behind me. The tide must have come in while I was watching the birds. I could swim but I remembered Princess saying something about really bad rip currents and how we shouldn't go out swimming by ourselves. I wasn't the greatest swimmer to begin with. The instructor at the Yardville pool had always smelled a little like pedophile and Annie and I would skip swim class and practice handstands in the shallow end. Screaming was probably a better solution.

"HELP!" I yelled with everything I had. All I did was startle the birds, who decided to stop falling for their fish around the jetty because the squawking lady was ruining their dinner.

"HELP, HELP, HELP. Anyone, please help."

But they were all laughing and drinking and partying indoors, and they thought I had gone to bed. No one was going to help.

But maybe there was hope.

There was a light bobbing up and down in the distance. It was a boat. I kept screaming, the salt water stinging the back of my throat. I tried to jump up and down but didn't want to lose my footing, so I did more knee bends and waved my arms like one of the Village People doing YMCA.

A white fishing boat with a small blue light on top captained by a portly man with a shock of dark hair pulled alongside the jetty that had become just a couple of rocks in the open ocean.

"*Buonasera, signora. Ciao, ciao. Come stai?*"

What was an Italian fisherman doing off the coast of Mexico? Not that I cared. I took his outstretched arm and climbed onto the little ledge of his boat. Under the blue light he took a better look at my face.

"Sophie," he said with a smile.

"What?"

"*Si era Sophie*. Sophie and Joe."

What was happening? Maybe I had passed out on the rocks and fallen into the ocean and drowned, and this was some weird limbo or heaven or hell or a fantasy world like Wonderland, except instead of a Cheshire Cat I had this large Italian gentleman to lead me on my journey.

"*Mi chiamo Pippo*," he said, drawing out the Pip like Peep. Pippo. Pippo? How did I know that name? Joe! I knew it because of Joe. Joe told me the story about Pippo, the cuckolded fisherman. Now Pippo was on his cell phone speaking in rapid-fire Italian. He handed me the phone.

"Joe," he proffered.

I grabbed it.

"Joe?"

"Sophie! Why are you in the middle of the ocean? Are you OK?"

"I just took a walk. I climbed out to the jetty and then the tide came and I got stuck and then Pippo came. Why is Pippo here?"

"Sophie, you're breaking up. I can't hear you. Come to shore."

Joe would be on the shore when I went back. That was good, and exciting. Of course, he may believe that I tried to drown myself, but I could explain all that away.

Pippo looked me over again. "Sophie," he said with a smile.

"Pippo," I said, smiling right back.

When we reached the sand, Joe was standing on the shore with a towel. I ran over to him.

Pippo stayed on the boat. Joe waved and yelled out what I assumed was a thank you in Italian.

He threw his arms around me.

"Sophie, why did you go out there?"

I couldn't help it; I buried my head in his neck and soaked in the smell of him.

"I just took a walk and then I saw the pelicans and I couldn't stop watching them. I think you're wrong not to want to be like a pelican. See, they aren't afraid of falling hard. They know what they want and they dive and they get it. I want you. I want to dive for you. I want to fall for you and I don't care if I get hurt. I love you."

I didn't know what he was going to say. But I didn't hold my breath and my stomach wasn't doing the knotty flip-flops.

215

Whatever the answer was I was going to be fine, but he had to know how I felt.

He leaned into me.

"Sophie, I already fell. You're my fish. The best one."

And then he kissed me and it's cheesy and corny to describe it like this but it was like no other kiss I had ever felt in my life. It was the kind of kiss you read about and the kind that old-time movie stars did in black-and-white films before getting on planes and leaving each other forever to be with some deadbeat spouse they didn't love.

When we finally broke apart after what had to be ten minutes, I looked up at him again.

"Pippo?"

He smiled. "Is my date for the wedding and the very first client of Love Rehab South."

"He's a client?"

"He is. He's part of a group of ten who will do the first love retreat after the wedding. What you did for the women—I think we can do that for a lot of people. Everyone is fucked up when it comes to love and romance. If we can only realize that we're all messed up in the same way, then we can get better."

"Do you think I'm better?"

"Do you think you're better?"

I got quiet. I wanted to be honest.

"I think I'm a work in progress."

He smiled again, and I knew I would never get tired of that smile.

"I think we all are, Sophie."

"Joe?" I asked tentatively. "Are you really leading me to believe that what happened tonight actually, really, and truly was just a hilarious misunderstanding?"

Joe belly laughed so hard he had to put his hands on his knees.

"There go your rules. You are living in a romantic comedy right now."

I was falling hard. It was both romantic *and* comedic.

It can happen, OK?

But I had to hit rock bottom before I was ready to do it. That was the part they never show you in romantic comedies, the picking yourself up after it all falls apart, when everything sucks for a good period of time.

I'll spare you the details. I don't want to be that person who gives anyone false hope or a practicum guide for how falling in love should and will work. Needless to say, Joe and I walked off the beach that night and had what can only be described as a year's worth of pent-up and rehabilitated orgasms.

Katrina and Tito blended Jewish, Mexican, and Mayan traditions into their ceremony, in addition to some things that were simply Katrina.

She asked that all the guests do a labyrinth walk before convening on the beach where they would be married by Rabbi Scheilman, who had flown down from the Upper West Side.

The labyrinth on the property was composed of stones laid in the sand. I watched my newfound friends, women and men whom, for the most part, I hadn't known at this time last year. They had all come into my life in varying states of disarray, most of them a little bit broken. But together we had healed one another. And I had been a big part of making that happen. I smiled as I watched all of them wend their way through the maze of stones, shoes mostly in hand, knowing they would more easily be able to wend their way through the twists and turns of life.

From the outside it looked like a maze, but once you walked into it you realized that it was just a single path that led to the center after a series of twists and turns had led you close and then farther away from your goal.

As Joe and I walked it hand in hand, I couldn't help but think that the labyrinth was like any relationship. Just when you think you're getting close to something, all of a sudden a twist or a turn can put you right back where you started. And that had to be OK, or you would never get to the good stuff.

Joe might be my soul mate; he might not be. But I was in love and I was happy and that was perfectly good enough for right now. I had serenity.

Acknowledgments

Authors like to lament the loneliness of their working life. Writing *Love Rehab* wasn't lonely at all for me. This book was inspired by more than a decade's worth of stories my girlfriends have told me about their love lives. While none of the characters are representative of any particular person I know, all of the characters are composites of people I love, so I felt as though I was surrounded by friends throughout the writing process.

So many people read early drafts of this novel. I want to thank a few of them (and for those of you that I leave out, I will buy you a cocktail or set you up with my cute single cousin sometime in the near future): Emily Foote, Ursula MacMullan, Leah Chernikoff, Leah Popowich, Samantha Prestia, Jackie Cascarano, Megan O'Brien (who insisted that I actually name a character using her real name), Tre Miller, Cooper Lawrence, Paula Froelich, and Christine Ryan.

Special thanks to my girlfriends from high school: Rebecca "Becky" Prusinowki, Andrea Pasquine, and Julia Fisher Nastasi, all of whom participated in many a late-night drive-by of one or another Holy Ghost boy's house when we were sixteen, and actually watched my high school boyfriend's *90210* video tape collection with me.

I dedicated this book to all the boyfriends who have inspired me to behave in ways unbecoming to a lady. I have a special place in my heart for each and every one of them, except for that one guy who cheated on me with thirty-seven women. I hope he got herpes.

I drank a lot of wine while writing this book, so I really want to thank the kind people at Wine.com for your impeccable service and moderately priced, full-bodied California reds.

I also aged a little bit throughout the process, so I want to thank Dr. Michael Reed for his laser focused Botox.

Of course, thanks to my wonderful editors: Jen Pooley, who never ceased to tell me that the book was awesome even when I felt like it wasn't anymore, and Nicole Passage, who knows that I do not know, where commas, should always, be.

Jane Friedman, Tina Pohlman, Rachel Chou, Mary Sorrick, and Libby Jordan from Open Road totally believed that I could write a novel and because of that, I actually did it.

And as always, John and Tracey. Thanks for messing me up just enough to have something to write about. Love you guys.

Need more
Love Rehab?

Check in here:

GetLoveRehab.com

Facebook.com/LoveRehabNovel

@LoveRehabNovel

Pinterest.com/LoveRehabNovel

EBOOKS BY JO PIAZZA

FROM OPEN ROAD MEDIA

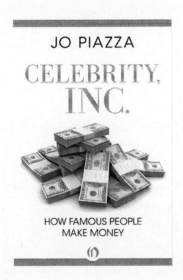

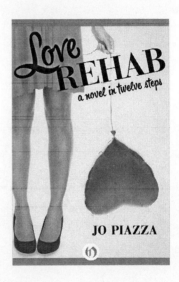

Available wherever ebooks are sold

OPEN ROAD

INTEGRATED MEDIA

Open Road Integrated Media is a digital publisher and multimedia content company. Open Road creates connections between authors and their audiences by marketing its ebooks through a new proprietary online platform, which uses premium video content and social media.

CPSIA information can be obtained at www.ICGtesting.com
Printed in the USA
BVOW072100240413

319059BV00002B/12/P